ROAD TO DISASTER

A WESTBAY CITY MYSTERY

AVA ZUMA

CLEANTALES PUBLISHING

OTHER BOOKS IN THE WESTBAY CITY SERIES

End of the Road

Hit the Road

Burn Up the Road

Road to Recovery

A WESTBAY CITY MYSTERY

BOOK TWO

1

———

As Luke Mbeki tore down Sandville Street, his legs carrying him faster than he had ever attempted, he felt his lungs were about to burst. His vision was getting blurred, and his breathing laboured. At any moment, he felt he could collapse on the hot tarmac.

If he didn't die from over-exerting himself, it would happen because of where he was. He had no business chasing down a thief in Sandville, because this was their haven. It was a neighbourhood in a seedy part of WestBay City, known to be one of the favoured hideouts for the city's criminals, both big and small.

He also hadn't factored in chasing suspected criminals as part of his job description when he started his private investigator business, something he had zero experience in. After the marketing agency he'd co-founded shut down after the death of his partner, Victor, he took a risk to start afresh. He had no choice. To add fuel to the fire, he'd just divorced his wife. In many quarters, a man in his early forties like himself wasn't supposed to start afresh. They were supposed to be coasting towards retirement. Yet here he was, exerting himself to rebuild his life. It was days like this that made him doubt if it was all going to pay off.

A newcomer like himself stood out in this neighbourhood. What made it so dangerous was chasing down a criminal on their home turf was unheard of. Often, if the criminal ventured into the neighbourhood, their pursuers stopped and turned back, counting their losses. Anyone down the street - which was dotted with hawkers, shops blaring loud music, a few battered cars, motorbikes, and groups of onlookers – could attack him.

He'd never been here before, and when the thief started running towards it, Luke second-guessed himself. Did he want to keep chasing this guy down for the bounty on his head and the client's pay? Was it worth his own life and security? He'd wanted a new start in life and some income, but several cases later, he realised he was possibly punching above his weight.

The thief had stolen some electronics from his boss' shop two weeks prior; armed with the key provided as a newly promoted shop supervisor, he loaded the pricey goods onto a *bakkie*, the cheapest old pickup truck he could find, and drove them off one night. The police hadn't made progress with the investigation, choosing to focus on other crimes, so Luke had taken over the job after the frustrated client called.

Tracking the fellow had taken four days. Luke had been patient, trawling e-commerce websites and working with Kabelo Mtanse, one of his three employees and the most street-smart, to trace the goods. They'd spotted one on a site and set up a meeting. They had just shown up and the culprit had realised they were there to confront him.

Kabelo had warned that he might start running towards Sandville, and maybe a location change would be ideal. The best they could do was to get the man to meet them across the street, where he had an escape route that he was now using.

Luke hadn't realised how much he'd fear the whole experience until he was already in the thick of the chase.

He then remembered his father's words from his childhood, said as they went out hunting one day: "**Akukho kufa kunjani**" his father told him. "No death is different, even that of a snake bite. So don't be afraid of it." Over the years, he'd come to appreciate what his father meant. If he met a snake while hunting a rabbit, he'd have to kill the snake before it killed him. But to do that, he had to let go of fear, for it would cloud his judgement.

Luke didn't see a snake nor did he kill the rabbit, but the lesson remained and he'd applied it in many situations. This one needed it.

Kabelo had taken another route, aiming to cut off the runner. He looked like a gladiator as he ran off, dressed in his trademark bike riders' leather jacket. Luke's was more muted in his jeans and t-shirt. His job was to keep chasing the man straight down the street and close him down. However, his body hadn't experienced such exertion in a long time, and he was struggling. The gap between him and the man grew wider.

Luke was almost giving up when, from one of the side alleys, Kabelo emerged and dived for the culprit's torso, tackling him to the ground.

The two men lay on the ground, catching their breath, Kabelo on top of the runner. Luke slowed down and took a moment to also catch his breath, arms akimbo. Seconds later, he lumbered towards them.

"Keep your hands on him. Don't let him go," Luke said in between pants.

By the time he got to them, the culprit was trying to get on his feet. Luke used the fact he was standing to overpower him. He and Kabelo held on to him as they waited for the police to arrive.

As this happened, small groups of men approached them.

"What's going on Kabs?" one man asked.

"Hey, we're just here to get our man," Kabelo replied.

"You're with the cops now?" the man said.

"No, we're not. Private investigators," Kabelo replied.

"Same thing. Who's he?" the man asked, pointing to Luke.

"He's with me. So don't sweat it," Kabelo said.

"You know we don't play with the cops, right?" the man remarked.

"I know. But he's not from here. So allow us to get him out and we'll be out of your hair," Kabelo said.

"How do you know he's not from here?" the man posed.

"You know me. Do you know him?" Kabelo asked. Luke knew Kabelo was testing the man's bluff. They eyed each other for a moment.

"We'll do that only because it's you," the man said.

They waited some more with the neighbourhood's men milling around them. Luke thought it was one of the most tension-filled waits he'd ever experienced.

When the police arrived, they handed him over. The man confessed to where the goods were hidden. Satisfied, Luke and Kabelo left the place.

When Luke called the client, he was ecstatic. He wired the investigation fee balance shortly afterwards.

"That was a hard earned pay day. Should we turn around and just head straight to the airport?" Luke joked as he drove on the M4 highway towards the office.

"Of course!" Kabelo replied. They laughed, the humour allowing them to expend some of the tension they had accumulated.

When they arrived at their office, they found Reggie Grey waiting. A balding man in his forties, he had come to Luke's office two weeks earlier, distraught. He'd been having a difficult time with his wife and wanted to know if she was cheating on him.

Today Reggie looked anxious, sitting on the edge of one of the plastic seats they had in the sparsely furnished office. It was on the third floor of the Kenesha Building, not the fanciest building in town, but decent enough for an upstart company like *L.M. Private Investigators.*

Kabelo went to the washroom as Luke attended to Reggie.

"Thank you for your patience, Reggie. Are you here for the video?" Luke asked.

"Yes, and to finalise the payment," Reggie replied.

Luke raised a brow. "We haven't finished the investigation. We agreed to follow your wife when she takes that business trip, remember?"

"That won't be necessary. The preview you sent yesterday was enough. I'm not going to drag this out any longer," Reggie replied.

Luke sighed. Reggie looked defeated, weighing the magnitude of finding out that his wife was cheating on him. Luke didn't like such cases, although they were more common in his line of work. They reminded him of Helen, his ex-wife. He wondered if she'd had an affair he never knew about. Frankly, he didn't want to know. He knew these kinds of thoughts plagued the minds of men who came to him seeking to investigate their wives. He didn't take pleasure in the misery his findings caused, but he had to learn how to separate his personal emotions from the work.

"Alright. I'm sorry that I was the bearer of bad news. Shall I pro-rate the fee?" Luke asked.

Reggie shook his head. "Not at all. I'll pay you the full fee we agreed on."

Luke shook his head. "Sir, I know you're not in a good place right now. That's a lot of money and I wouldn't like to take advantage of you at this sensitive time."

"Cut the hogwash. I'm giving you the full fee. Consider it a bonus for the good work," Reggie said. He took out his cheque and a pen and filled in the blanks.

When the cheque got into Luke's hands, the zeros jumped off the page and fantasies of what he could do with the extra cash flashed across his mind. Reggie was a man of means, and it was another big payment into the firm's business account. For Luke, this was one of their most productive periods since they opened six months ago.

"I appreciate the payment. But take some time out. Think about what you'll do next. It's better you set aside the emotions and let your head rule. It will make things smoother for you," Luke said.

"Thanks again for your help," Reggie said as he stood and adjusted his belt.

"What are you going to do now?" Luke asked.

Reggie sighed and then shrugged. "I was thinking of kicking her out the minute I got home. But after your advice, I'll still ask her to leave but in a more measured manner. At least I'll try to."

"Please do. I always tell my clients that their spouse has already brought enough misery in their life. Getting arrested will only make them win. Don't do it. Give yourself the chance to start again on a clean slate," Luke said.

"Wise words. That's what I'll keep in mind because I'm still angry, you know," Reggie said.

"I know. Take care of yourself, sir," Luke replied.

Reggie left and Luke sat alone in the office. He held up the cheque.

"You keep surprising me every day," Luke said.

"Who does?" Cindi Twala, his operations manager, asked as she strode in.

In her hands were two bags filled with stationery. Behind her, Kabelo followed. He was carrying a heavy carton, which he placed on an empty table next to the door.

"Another case closed," Luke said. "That's the printer?"

"*Yebo*. Cheapest I could get," Cindi replied. "Looks like we just got paid judging from your smile."

"You know me too well," Luke replied. She reached for the cheque and briefly studied it. Her eyes widened.

"He gave a fifty percent tip on top of the fee?" she asked.

"Your eyes aren't lying. This was a good one," Luke said.

She looked up at him. "You realise we broke even two cases ago?"

"This little experiment is going better than expected," Luke said. "Maybe the collapse of FZ marketing was a blessing."

Kabelo shook his head. "No, boss. That was a dark time. You can't say it was a blessing losing your own business like that. No."

"I agree with Kabs. We don't have to deny it was a tough time," Cindi said.

"Alright, alright. I agree it wasn't great. Heck, I even get flashbacks. But to be honest, I felt this was going to be tougher than that was," Luke said.

"We've been watching you and we know it's been tough, so relax," Kabelo said.

Luke chuckled. "That's one of the things that made me take the plunge. Knowing you two have my back."

"Don't butter us up like that," Cindi said.

"It's true!" Luke said. "But we're all fighters. Taking it a day at a time was the smart choice, because together we're good at this thing."

"You're making the best of your snooping nature at least," Cindi said with a wink.

"So, are we celebrating or what?" Kabelo asked.

"Not so fast. Look around us. What's this place look like?" Cindi said.

Luke's eyes scanned the room. It was sizeable, capable of hosting seven people with the two tables and two plastic seats in it. But that was all it had, and it hardly felt like an office.

"We said we'd upgrade things when we got here, didn't we?" Cindi asked.

"We sure did, but we're managing, aren't we?" Luke asked.

"Barely," Cindi said. "We need proper furniture."

"But we're getting good deals without it. It's not about the furniture, but about how we deliver," Luke replied.

"What if better seats and workspace leads to better clients with deeper pockets?" Cindi asked.

"Nah. Besides, I also need to move into my apartment, and I've got no furniture. At least this space can handle it. My apartment can't," Luke said. He'd lived at a cheap motel for so long, he'd become tired of the whole situation.

"Your business will fill your apartment, not the other way round," Cindi replied.

"Can we talk about this while having a good time somewhere?" Kabelo interjected.

Almost in unison, Luke and Cindi said. "No!"

Kabelo shook his head.

"I can understand you wanting to make the office better, but can't you see how me living in a decent place is good for my morale?" Luke asked.

"Are you taking us in as your roommates?" Cindi posed.

Luke frowned. "No way. Why would I do that?"

"That won't motivate us either since we're not connected to the space," Cindi replied.

"Then I'll have to make more money to get both our projects off the ground," Luke said.

There was a knock on the open door. The three turned to see who it was.

Standing in the doorway was a beautiful woman in her mid-thirties. She wore sunglasses, a sleeveless blue dress that stopped short of her knees. She had matching high heels, glowing skin and lush red lips that simmered in the light.

"Are you the private investigator?" she asked, staring at Luke.

"Yes, how may we help you?" Luke replied.

"I need to see you. Sorry, are you already in a meeting?" she asked.

Luke wondered why some people do that: disrupt a conversation without warning and then feign modesty.

"Not at all. These are members of my team. Kabelo over there and Cindi over here," Luke said, pointing them out.

The woman took off her glasses. Her eyes were crimson, as if she hadn't slept for a week.

"Great. Can I come in? I need you to help me find someone that's gone missing. And I think my life maybe in danger," she said with her voice cracking.

2

———————

LUKE APPRECIATED that Lynda was attractive. He noticed other details apart from her classy dressing. He liked her well-done nails, natural hair, poise, and manner of speaking. However, he had long since decided he wouldn't fraternise with clients, no matter how inviting it looked or flirtatious they were. And he had encountered the flirty ones in several cases, and it wasn't always easy to keep them at bay. Often, he had to make sure Cindi was close by to discourage their advances. They tended to play nice when another female was present.

Lynda took a seat on the visitors' plastic seat. She didn't look bothered by this, which told him that although she had good taste, she didn't mind grafting to get results.

"Who's gone missing?" Luke asked.

"My husband. It's been three days and I have no idea where he is," Lynda replied.

"Tell us slowly what happened," Luke said as he flipped open a notebook and grabbed a pen.

Lynda took a deep breath.

"It was a regular day. He left for work and I stayed home doing... You know, stuff that housewives do," Lynda began.

"You don't work?" Luke asked.

"Being a housewife is work, you know," Lynda countered.

"My apologies, I didn't mean to offend. I meant to ask, you're not employed?" Luke said.

"No, I'm not. Mark wouldn't allow that. He always said he wanted us to build a home together, and I was a homemaker. We've been doing that for the past five years. Anyway, three days ago he left for work and I stayed home. We planned to have dinner together later that day. I have a pottery class that I take so in the afternoon I attended it for two hours, then drove back home to make dinner. Then the wait began. He didn't come home that day," Lynda said.

"Did he call you to say anything?" Cindi asked.

"No, nothing. Radio silence. I called him a few times. His phone rang but he never took it. When I called him the next day, his phone was off," she replied.

"What business does he run?" Cindi asked.

"He owns Mach 1 Couriers. It's a successful company and has grown a lot in the last three years," she said.

"I've seen their vans around town. Did you check with the office?" he asked.

"They told me he had a special package to deliver that afternoon. They didn't tell me where," Lynda replied.

"He makes some deliveries himself?" he asked, frowning.

Lynda nodded. "Yes. He has some high-profile clients who prefer to receive deliveries from him."

"I've never heard of that before," Luke said. "Have you informed the police?"

"I went there the next day. They said I had to wait a bit

more. Especially when I told them he's been away a few times and returned," Lynda replied.

"Hold on. He's done this before?" Luke asked.

"Kind of. He sometimes goes on short trips, then returns. He doesn't always tell me beforehand. But we've never made plans like this and then he doesn't show up," she replied.

"I see. Did he have any enemies?" Luke asked.

"None that I know of," Lynda replied. "Look, I need to know if you can help me here."

Luke smiled. "I think we can."

He glanced at Cindi, who frowned at him. He ignored her.

"Listen. If I take this on, I'll need you to be honest with me about everything you know about Mark and the day he disappeared. I might ask you some questions you've never asked yourself to get to the bottom of things. Are you okay with that?" Luke asked.

Lynda nodded. "I'm okay with that. I just want him to be found as soon as possible. How long will it take you?"

"Probably the next forty-eight hours," Luke replied.

Luke noticed Cindi's jaw dropping as she raised her eyebrows. He knew she didn't like him making such promises, but he felt bullish.

"That's great. If you can find him even sooner, the better. I'm ready to pay you a good sum for him. Provided he comes safe," Lynda said, reaching into her bag and taking out a cheque book. "How much will this cost?"

Luke leaned back in his chair. "Well, you'll be paying me per hour each time I'm in the field. By the look of things, we might not need accommodation or flights because he might be in the locality, so..."

"But we're not sure, of course. So we may keep you posted on the actual cost," Cindi interjected.

Lynda pursed her lips. "Oh, I thought you'd just give me a ballpark figure first, then revise it from there."

Luke cleared his throat. "Well, a ballpark figure will…"

"Will need to discuss that. Luke, can we talk about it outside?" Cindi asked.

Not wanting to cause a scene, Luke nodded.

"Just give us five minutes, we'll be right back," Luke said as he and Cindi stepped out into the reception area. There was no one else there.

"What do you think you're doing?" Cindi asked.

"What do you mean?" Luke asked.

"You've not shown her the terms and conditions document we ask every client to sign before we start. You've not given us time to know her better and set a rate. You just want to give her a ballpark figure?" Cindi asked.

"You're overthinking this. Her husband is missing, and it's been over forty-eight hours. You know how crucial the first forty-eight hours are. Why should we hold back?" Luke asked.

"I've not told you to hold back. I'm simply saying to find out a little more about her. You don't even know where she lives. You're rushing this more than other cases we've done," Cindi said.

"Only because a missing person's report is serious. Anything could be happening to him and we're here making conversation. We need to get out and start looking for him. What could go wrong?" Luke said.

"Remember the Carlson case? The one we thought was simply a teen running away from home and then we had to go all the way to Jo'burg to get him? His father didn't like the extra costs. What if the case needs us to go out of town? What then? If you give her a blanket figure and then add more costs to it, it might get complicated. Remember, she's housewife, not a banker," Cindi said.

"She might have access to the account to move around, no? That shouldn't worry you. She looks like she's keeping an open mind about the whole thing," Luke said.

"Can you at least hold out on the projections before we understand our scope? Just to make things easier for us?" Cindi asked.

"We'll be fine. If she wants to pay now, all we have to do is get a deposit. We'll then add the rest after we gain more info," Luke said.

"So you don't want her to sign the document now like we usually do?" Cindi asked.

"It will happen eventually. It always does," he said.

Cindi sighed. "I think you're rushing to close the deal because of the cash, or she's distracting you."

Luke raised a brow. "Distracting me?... how?"

"She's attractive, or you want to deny that too?" she asked.

"That's not even crossed my mind until now," Luke protested.

"Oh, come on, Luke," Cindi said, but he grabbed her arm.

"Sssh!" Luke said. They both went quiet. "Can you hear that?"

Lynda's voice filtered into the hallway. She sounded agitated.

Luke opened the office door and found Lynda talking on her mobile phone.

"I can't do that. I seriously can't do that. Please tell me where he is," Lynda said, her eyes tearing. "Hello? Hello?"

Lynda lowered her phone.

"Who was that?" Luke asked.

Lynda shook her head. "I don't know. He had one of those robotic voices. He says he can tell me where Mark is if I agree to do as he says."

"And what does he want you to do?" Luke asked.

"To give him five hundred thousand rand," Lynda replied.

3

———————

Luke had heard of a few crazy ransom requests, but not this crazy. This was the strangest one yet. He frowned and reached for her phone. She handed it over with a trembling hand. The caller number was private.

He looked up at Lynda's distraught face. "That doesn't make any sense. How's finding Mark supposed to help you if you agree to kill yourself?"

Lynda didn't respond. Instead, she sniffled, took out a handkerchief and dried her eyes.

"Does anyone else know about Mark's disappearance?" Cindi asked.

"Other than the police, no one else at the moment," Lynda replied.

"Are you sure? Not even your close friends?" Luke asked.

"Only Edna. She advised me it was still too soon to tell if he's missing or not. I can't go spreading alarm everywhere. I was thinking of letting other people know later today, now that I'm talking to you. Why?" Lynda said.

"Just narrowing the possibilities," he said. "Who's Edna?"

"An old friend from university. She lives in Cape Town but we keep in touch. What possibilities?" Lynda said.

"That the person who took him isn't someone close to you," Luke replied.

Lynda's eyes widened. "Do you think it's one of our friends?"

"Or relatives. Anything is possible," Luke replied. "Do you mind if I visit your home? It can help me get a clearer picture of things."

"Oh. Yeah, sure. I can take you," a flustered Lynda replied. "What about the fee?"

"Let's talk about that after I visit your home," Luke said.

"Alright. Let's go," Lynda said. She walked to the door.

"I'm coming too," Cindi said, grabbing her bag.

"What about the office?" Luke asked.

"Kabelo will look after things," Cindi replied.

Luke knew Kabelo wanted to go out on a ride but wasn't surprised when Cindi convinced him to change his plans. Working with him during their marketing agency days had taught her how to sell water to a fish.

They drove to the Melberg Estates, a chain of standalone homes within a gated community owned by the middle class. Each home had its own design, but the driveway leading up to each house was the same, lined with short trees and fancily trimmed bushes. They arrived at the gate of House 53. Lynda parked her Volkswagen GTI next to an empty parking space, which Luke assumed belonged to Mark's car. Luke parked his car in a visitor's parking space outside the gate.

"Will you have tea or wine?" Lynda asked once they were inside.

"Nothing for me," Luke said.

"Same here," Cindi added.

"No, I can't allow that. My mother raised me to serve my visitors, so even a sip will be acceptable. I'll stir up some ginger tea. It will only take five minutes," Lynda replied and disappeared into the kitchen.

Luke gave the room a once over. It was minimalist in style, but still had colourful framed photographs on each wall: a kestrel on one, an eagle on another, a peregrine falcon on a third. He walked over to the mantelpiece and saw the single photograph in the room of Mark and Lynda smiling in a photo studio. It was airbrushed and saturated to add to its richness, and Luke thought they'd make great magazine cover models. Mark looked lean and sharply dressed in a suit. He sported a well-trimmed beard that enhanced the aura of authority around him.

"They look happy," Cindi said, standing next to him.

"You think their love is real or artificial?" Luke asked.

"Touched up photos always make it look artificial. It's not a fair measure of things. I think it's real," she replied.

"Fair enough. But what do the eyes tell you?" Luke asked.

"The eyes?" Cindi asked.

"Yes. They can touch up the skin, the colours, the outfits, but most times they leave the eyes. You know what they say - they are the windows to the soul. So I look at them to find some truth in the image," Luke said.

"What are they telling you?" Cindi asked.

"I asked you first," he replied.

Cindi sighed and studied the image. "They once knew a deep love, but it's fading. At least in his eyes. Maybe the business took over."

"Or another woman," Luke said.

"He doesn't look like the type," Cindi said.

"There's nothing logical in these situations. Things happen," Luke replied.

They both heard the clink of mugs placed on a tray and turned just in time to see Lynda coming back. On the tray were two steaming mugs of tea and a plate of rusk biscuits.

"I told you it wouldn't take long," Lynda said as she placed the tray on the coffee table. Luke and Cindi took their mugs of tea and settled in their seats.

"We were looking at the photo of you and your husband there. Is it recent?" Luke asked.

"Ah no, it's about a year old. Mark has grown bigger since then. I've been feeding him better than usual," Lynda remarked.

"Really? Why is that?" Luke asked.

"It's one of our love languages. I love cooking, he enjoys eating it. Perfect combo," she said.

"Has everything been going well between the two of you?" Luke asked.

"It hasn't been perfect. But we talk and thrash out anything that needs to be fixed. That's why we're still together after five years," Lynda said.

"Do you have any kids?" Cindi asked.

Lynda shook her head. "We never wanted one for a while after we got married. It was a mutual decision. But we talked about it recently and now that the business has taken off, we're ready. He does have a child from another relationship."

Luke's eyes widened. "He does? How old is the child?"

"A fourteen-year-old boy. It was with his first love," Lynda replied.

"Does Mark visit him?" Cindi asked.

"Yeah, every so often. He's even come here a few times," Lynda said.

"And how does he respond to you?" Luke prodded.

Lynda inhaled. "It will take some getting used to, but we're not rushing him into anything."

"Fair enough. How do you get on with his mother?" Luke asked.

Lynda paused for a moment. "Faith and Mark get on as best as co-parents can. It's cordial. I don't care about those things. I just want my marriage to work."

"You don't care about the situation with his ex?" Luke queried.

Lynda shrugged. "I care if it affects him. But it doesn't faze me. We go with the flow and make the most of things as they are."

Luke grunted. He could sense a frosty relationship between Lynda and Faith, but he needed more time to confirm it.

"I see. Did you have an argument or disagreement with Mark before he disappeared?" Luke asked.

"Not at all. Like I said, we were planning to have dinner later that day," Lynda replied.

"I'm guessing you've been worried since the day he didn't turn up. Why haven't you told more people?" Cindi asked. Luke nodded, for it was a question he wanted to ask.

"I wasn't sure how to handle it. He's disappeared for a few days at a time. But he always texts me after a day or two," she replied.

"So what makes you think he's not doing the same thing?" Luke asked.

"After the pottery class, we were supposed to have dinner. Even on our worst days, cancelling a date is done by letting the other person know. He didn't do it this time and I haven't heard from him since. Not even a text letting me know where he is," Lynda replied.

"So, what did you do that night?" Luke asked.

"I couldn't sleep. I kept wondering what was going on and where he could be. My curiosity drove me to look through his pockets and documents. I know it sounds a little crazy, but I was worried," Lynda said. "And I found something."

Luke leaned forward. "What did you find?"

"Just give me a sec. I'll show you," Lynda replied. She stood up and went up the stairs towards the master bedroom.

Luke and Cindi exchanged glances.

"What do you think?" Luke asked.

"Interesting story so far. I've found no reason to doubt her. You?" Cindi said.

"Same here. But let's see what she comes with," Luke said.

Soon after, Lynda returned. She had two documents in her hand. She handed him the first one.

"This is an air ticket he booked for the next day. He was going to fly out to Mpumalanga. I didn't know why because he'd never been there before, and he never mentioned this trip," Lynda said.

"You know no one from there he might want to see?" Luke asked.

Lynda shook her head. "None."

Luke studied the ticket.

"Then there is this other one," Lynda said as she gave him the second document. It was a typed letter.

Luke read the letter, which was just two paragraphs long.

'Dear M and L,

You know I've been waiting for my request to be honoured but you're dragging your feet. I can't sustain myself forever on your hand-outs. Here's a simple solution: give me six months' worth of salary and I'll get out of your hair forever.

If not, all bets are off. Don't drive me to the edge. Let's avoid that. We all want to see the end of the year, don't we? Act accordingly.

Yours, G.'

"Who on earth is G?" Luke asked.

"A former employee that Mark had to fire. Mark said his name is George. George West," Lynda replied.

"Why is he sending you this letter?" Cindi asked.

Lynda sighed. "It's a long story. To summarise, he believes Mark was wrong to fire him and wants his job back. He's stalked and threatened him several times, but that's about it."

"That's not all," Luke said.

"What do you mean?" she asked.

"His sentence is interesting: 'we all want to see the end of the year.' That's not just a sentence. That's a threat," Luke said.

Lynda's eyes narrowed. "What do you mean?"

"This man might know where your husband is. Hopefully, he's not harmed him. We need to find George. Now," Luke replied.

4

———————

"I PRAY that this turns out to be nothing more than a husband who went for some alone time," Luke said to himself as he drove into the Mach 1 office compound. He didn't want to think of a dire outcome. One has to hope to keep the mind alive.

The Mach 1 offices were housed in a two-floor stone building painted white and blue. Emblazoned across the side of the building was the name 'Mach 1'. Luke figured it was a clever adaptation of Mark's name.

Parked outside were several vans and motorcycles branded in company colours. He made his way to the reception, which was a simple yet stylish affair with a chrome-coloured reception desk and a bespectacled woman in a company polo shirt, smiling at him.

"Good morning, sir. How may I help you?" the receptionist said.

"I'm here on behalf of Lynda Stone. I'd like to see Freddie, the manager," Luke said.

The receptionist called him, and moments later, the manager appeared.

Freddie Vumisa was a heavyset man with a casual gait. He gave Luke a firm handshake that lingered a little longer than necessary.

"Lynda told me you'd be coming. What do you want to know?" Freddie asked.

"Could you give me a brief rundown of your clientele?" Luke asked.

"We have two classes of clients: the regular and the VIP," Freddie replied. "The regular clients receive deliveries via the vans and motorcycles. However, Mark always paid extra attention to the VIP deliveries. These were handled by a driver called Melvin or by Mark himself. In special instances, he'd even use his personal vehicle to deliver to these high-profile clients."

"Are they all repeat clients?" Luke asked.

"Over seventy percent are. Some clients were only known to Mark and had only their initials indicated in the books. On the day he disappeared, Mark was running a secret high profile errand," Freddie said.

"Can I see the delivery notes?" Luke asked.

"We sometimes don't do those. But we do record each dispatch," Freddie said.

He showed Luke a black book with listed names. Some entries were initials only. For that day, the entry was the initials B.C. and the address to a local hotel, the Sapphire. Luke jotted this down.

"I'm told that Mark has also been dealing with a difficult former employee. Do you know something about that?" Luke asked.

"You mean George?" Freddie asked. "He's a loose cannon."

"Loose in what way?" Luke asked.

"He's never gotten over the fact he messed up. He's

called here several times to lament. Came back in person about three times but stopped at the gate by security. He's the reason Mark handles some of the VIP deliveries," Freddie replied.

"What did he mess up?" Luke queried.

"He was to deliver a VIP package that never got to its destination," Freddie said.

"What was in the package and who was the client?" Luke asked.

Freddie shrugged. "We only know the initials. Nothing more. For the package, you'll have to ask Mark when he returns."

Luke found it odd that there was such secrecy to some deliveries. It gave room for underhand dealings. Although tempted, Luke didn't want to prompt Freddie that his boss might be missing, since Freddie didn't seem worried about Mark's absence. His brief was to help Luke with any information he asked for, which he was doing well so far.

"Do you have George's address?" Luke asked.

"He used to live at Fuzu flats, but he moved after he lost his job. I have no idea where he lives now," Freddie said.

"Great, thanks for this," Luke said.

"What did Lynda say you need this for again?" Freddie asked.

"Just an organisational audit. I help with business strategy," Luke said.

"Does Mark know?" Freddie asked.

"Of course. That's why Lynda called you to help me out," Luke lied.

Freddie smiled. "Great. If you need anything else, just call me."

Freddie handed Luke his business card, but Luke didn't return the favour. Cindi always complained that they didn't have business cards. In this case, even if he had one, Luke wouldn't have given it to Freddie unless it had a fake title.

Luke was walking back to the car when his phone rang. It was Lynda.

"How did it go?" she asked.

"Very well, I had no hiccups," Luke replied.

"Great. I just found out something that you need to know," Lynda said. "Mark's gun is missing."

Luke stopped walking. "Hold on. What do you mean, gun?"

"Mark has a shooting rifle. He goes hunting or shooting practise. It's gone," Lynda said.

"Does he have any other guns?" Luke asked.

"No, that's the only one. It never leaves unless he plans to go to the shooting range," she said.

"You said it's a rifle," Luke said.

"Yes, the one with a long barrel. I don't know much about guns, so I can't tell you the make," Lynda said.

He asked for the shooting range address and she gave it to him.

After the call, Luke sat in his car for a few minutes. Had George waylaid Mark and kidnapped him at the shooting range or while he made the delivery? Did the delivery reach its destination? Did Mark take the gun for security reasons?

The engine roared to life and he pulled out of the car park, heading towards the shooting range.

It was a forty-five minute drive to the Westfield shooting range, which made it ideal if Mark wanted to go for a quick break and shoot some targets.

The drive there was uneventful. It was right on the edge of the city. He noted the shift from high-rises to single floor buildings and eventually open fields. The tree-lined roads made it a relaxing drive. He didn't even need music; the steady drone of his engine was enough.

As he got closer to the location, he looked out for the old rusted sign he was told about. He saw it to the left, dangling on the ends of two dog chains, swaying in the breeze. He turned onto a dirt road that was flanked by tall grass on both sides. As he drove, he kicked up a cloud of dust so big he couldn't see anything in his rear-view mirror.

He arrived at a low wrought-iron gate. He waited and realized there was no one coming to open it. Luke got out, found that the gate wasn't padlocked, and opened it. He closed it after getting in and drove for another five minutes before he saw an old stone building. It had a gravel car park next to it and he came to a stop there.

"Hello! Anybody home?" he asked as he went to the rickety wooden door of the building. It was locked. On the porch he saw an empty chalkboard with 'shooting order' painted in white atop it. But there were no names or shooting times indicated. He did a casual walk around the building and it was evident it hadn't been occupied for a few weeks.

"Did they go out of business?" he mused.

From the porch, he could see an open field and he made out shooting targets partially hidden by the brush.

He decided to check out the layout of the shooting range itself. If Mark used to come here, was he the only shooter who used the place? Luke kept a keen eye on his surroundings, lest the tall grass hid a gunman doing some target practice.

The shooting targets were of two different types: two human-shaped steel targets which were shot up to the point one of them was bent in half. These were older, and in his view, already retired. The reactive steel targets were newer and looked like a plant stalk with round leaves as targets. He touched them and they could move if hit. He figured the clang sound a bullet strike made felt satisfying to a shooter.

It made him think: did he need a gun as an investigator? Other than his first case with Chris Kalala and the Mestope case where he had to find an armed fugitive, this was only the third case involving guns. Maybe if he found Mark, he could get introduced to the process of gun ownership. He'd decide then.

He combed the shooting range, looking for any clue he could find. The place was clean, with no litter that caught his eye or gave a sign of Mark's presence.

An hour later, he had covered the shooting range, the area around the house and car park.

He scanned the area one more time and realised that beyond the shooting range was more thick brush. However, he was hesitant to check it out – any creature could be living there, including snakes.

After weighing the odds, he decided he'd give the area a quick look, not venturing too far lest he got into a tricky situation. He put on his jacket to prevent scratching his skin on branches, and ventured into the brush. He waded through it, parting tall grass and low-hanging branches as he scanned the area. The deeper he went, the more he encountered a swampy area with red mud. He stopped and saw there were at least two other sets of footprints that had walked through the same spot. He rubbed it off his shoes using the tall grass.

He slowly made his way through the thick bush. He'd pause momentarily to sense any suspicious movement as well as look for signs of disturbance. He didn't have any tracking skills of repute, relying on the few lessons his father taught when searching for something in similar terrain.

"Look out for broken twigs. Footprints. A torn cloth on a branch. Even blood rubbed off against a bark or leaf," his father had said.

This was one of the few memories he remembered of conversations with his father. He'd been a quiet man who rarely taught his son much, often spending time with his drinking buddies or watching football.

Luke's nostrils caught the whiff of a foul smell.

"This is why I didn't want to do this," he muttered to himself, imagining it was a dead, wild dog. Still he trudged on, the smell getting stronger, and he covered his nose.

Then he saw a shoe. It was a Cayman edition leather shoe, which was coated in dust. Its soles had traces of red mud. His heart started racing.

Two steps later, he found his answer. First, the intense smell hit his nose like a gut punch, although his hand still covered his nose. Flies were all over the place. On the ground, covered with some branches, lay a man in a dark suit. One of his shoes was missing.

His white shirt was caked in blood due to an open chest wound, where the flies were congregating. Suddenly, Luke's head felt light and his world spun. Something rose in his chest, and he leaned over as the contents of his bowel sped through his throat and mouth and onto the ground. He retched violently for a few minutes until his head hurt.

He had seen dead bodies, but none in this condition, in such a place. Mark had been thrown to the wild, never to be seen again.

It took him a few more minutes to regain his composure. He walked back to where the body was. Gathering courage, he lifted the branches off the body's face, and saw Mark's puffy, lifeless face.

He took a step back and that was when he saw the pistol. It was masked by one of the branches. Luke threaded a stick through the trigger hole and raised the pistol. It was a small firearm, with a gold-plated exterior and wooden handle. He could tell it was old, but unsure by how much.

Suddenly, he heard a movement behind him. He had only half-turned when a voice barked at him.

"Put the gun down and fall to your knees!"

Luke froze. "What?"

"I said put the gun down and fall to your knees. Now!" the voice barked again.

Luke let go of the stick, and the gun fell to the grass. He slowly lowered himself to the ground, inches from Mark's corpse.

Feet rushed toward him, and someone aggressively grabbed both his arms. Luke felt the cold, hard texture of handcuffs gripping his wrists.

"You're under arrest for the murder of Mark Stone. Anything you say or do..." a voice said.

That's all he remembered. The rest was a blur as he struggled to understand what was happening.

5

———————

Luke had a parched throat, but quenching his thirst was the last thing on his mind.

He sat on the ground, his back against the wheel of one of the police cars. He'd refused to get into the car, suspecting that if he got into the backseat, he'd be driven away to the station. Opting to sit on the ground until the lead detective arrived, his plan was to plead his case early: he was in the right place at the wrong time.

Luke shook his head as he stared at his dusty, scuffed shoes. Cindi's words of warning returned to him, and a wave of regret washed over him. Maybe she was right. He had rushed into this case without looking out for the red flags. Had he been set up? The last thing he needed was to be tied to a murder case just when his agency was picking up pace.

"I have to do better," he muttered to himself.

He needed to discipline himself, to fix his mental blind spots if he was going to make it in this business. He just hoped he hadn't made an irreparable error.

Luke fixated his eyes on the crime scene as detectives combed the scene for clues. They had sealed off with yellow tape the area where the body was found, and glove-wearing investigators filled several evidence bags with various objects of interest. The one piece of evidence that troubled Luke the most was the gun. Although he hadn't touched it, he felt like he had. He believed he had to explain why he was there before the police came up with their own theory.

Luke had settled his focus on Detective Tony and his partner, Detective Shozi, who were part of the investigation team. He knew Tony was more understanding than Shozi- she was quite militant towards him. Getting Tony on his side was key.

When he saw both detectives walking towards him, Luke tried to stand. However, this wasn't possible with his hands cuffed behind his back.

"What are you doing here, Luke?" Detective Tony asked.

"I was on the job as part of a search effort to find the deceased," Luke said.

"So you're still doing this private investigator thing?" Detective Tony asked.

Luke could detect the condescending tone in the detective's question, but he didn't want to rile them by calling it out.

"Yes. It's growing. Baby steps," Luke replied.

"Sounds like you found him," Detective Shozi said, making a mocking gesture to the word 'found' with her hands.

"He's been missing for a couple of days, and my client hired me to find him. I was simply lucky," Luke said.

"Which client is this?" Detective Tony asked.

"His wife," Luke replied.

Detective Tony and Shozi exchanged glances.

"Interesting. So you're telling us you had nothing to do with his death?" Detective Tony asked.

"Absolutely nothing. I swear over...," Luke said.

"Stop it right there. You don't have to swear over anything. Just tell us what we need to know," Detective Tony said. "When did you start your investigation?"

Detective Tony took out a small notebook that fit in the palm of his hand.

"Over twenty-four hours ago now," Luke replied.

Detective Tony paused and stared at him. "Twenty-four hours? You must be a bloodhound, or know more than you're telling me."

"I'm neither of those. I'm lucky, that's all. His wife Lynda came to my office and told us her situation," Luke said. "After asking her a few more questions, we agreed to a deal."

"And the deal was just to find him?" Detective Shozi asked.

"That's all there is to it, honestly," Luke said.

Just then, a uniformed policeman came into view behind the detectives. In his gloved hands were several large trash bags. Luke's eyes narrowed as the policeman arrived.

"Excuse me, detective. Have a look at this," the policeman said.

Detectives Tony and Shozi turned as the policeman started unfurling the trash bags to their full size. The policeman held them up by his side, and, to Luke's surprise, the trash bags were nearly human-size. His eyes widened at the same time as those of the detectives.

"Where did you get those?" Detective Shozi asked.

"They were in the boot of his car," the policeman replied. "Alongside other household supplies like buckets, shovels, duct tape."

The detectives turned back to Luke.

"What are these for?" Detective Tony asked.

"I'm getting ready to move into an apartment, so I did some shopping for it a few days ago," Luke replied.

"Why are they still in your boot days later? Were you trying to move the body?" Detective Shozi asked.

Luke shook his head. "No, no! It's my new house shopping. I always forget to take them out. I didn't want the trouble of taking them up to the motel room, then back down again when I'm ready."

"Tell us the truth," Detective Shozi said.

"It's the whole truth," Luke replied.

Detective Tony motioned to the policeman. "Help him inside."

The policeman helped Luke into the backseat of the police car. He was soon on the highway, heading to the station. Half an hour later, he was alone in a cold, poorly lit interrogation room surrounded by grey walls. They didn't cuff his hands to the small, austere metal table in front of him. All he could hear, seated all alone in the room, was the sound of his heavy breathing.

Moments later, Detective Tony entered the room.

"Have you thought about anything you might have forgotten?" Detective Tony asked.

"I have nothing to add," Luke said.

Detective Tony sighed. "Alright. You'll be spending the night in the cells."

Luke frowned. "Why?"

"We need to wait for some test results. I hope, for your sake, none of them connects this murder to you," the detective replied.

Sure enough, they led Luke to his cell. It was stuffy and had a lingering, unpleasant smell. After a few minutes, his nose got used to it. They brought food to him - a miserly mealie pap with vegetable and light meat stew - which he didn't have an appetite for. He slept in fits shortly afterwards, as the thin mattress offered little comfort.

He was up early the next day and watched streaks of light from the sun filter in through the high, grilled window, filling the cell.

He didn't have the porridge breakfast they offered.

It wasn't until the afternoon that he was taken to the interrogation room. He found Detective Tony and Shozi seated, waiting for him. On the table in front of them were two brown envelopes.

"Did you get some sleep?" Detective Tony asked.

"As much as a dodgy cell allows," Luke said.

"Good. We have some questions. We've just received the postmortem results. The victim was killed five days ago. Where were you five days ago?" Detective Tony asked.

Luke paused as he considered his answer. Then his eyes brightened.

"I was at a conference," Luke said. "It was a one-day conference for private investigators."

"Where was the conference?" Detective Tony asked.

"On the outskirts of town, at the Hotel Regent. It was a one-day affair, so I drove really early to get there before eight, then drove back and got to the motel after dark," Luke replied. "The Private Investigators' Association organised it."

"Shozi, please find out if his story checks out," Detective Tony instructed.

"Sure thing," Detective Shozi said. She left the room.

They sat in awkward silence for close to ten minutes.

"We're going to sit here and wait until she returns?" Luke asked.

"Exactly," Detective Tony replied. He spent that time reading the documents he took out from the envelope. Luke couldn't tell if they were for the present case or another one.

Detective Tony grunted. "I can allow you one call. Hopefully, there's someone who wants to bail you out."

"On which phone?" Luke asked.

"There's one on the wall there. In the corner," Detective Tony said.

Luke turned and saw a small locked box.

"You've got the key?" Luke asked.

Detective Tony chuckled. "I was joking. It's no longer in use. This is what you can use." He took out a mobile phone from his pocket and handed it to Luke.

"Is it tracked?" Luke asked.

"That's the least of your worries right now. Just make the call."

Luke held the phone in his hands, studying it. It was a basic one without internet.

He dialled Cindi's number, but the call didn't go through. Who else could he call? He wanted to call his mother, but she'd recently replaced her line and he hadn't memorised it yet. Kabelo was the other option, but he couldn't remember his phone number either. His list of choices settled on Helen, his ex-wife.

"Hello?"

"Hey, Helen. It's' Luke," he said.

"Why have you changed your number?" she asked.

"I haven't. I'm at the police station and might need some bail. Are you willing to come through if I need it? I'll refund you," Luke said.

Luke was greeted with silence, which seemed to linger for an eternity.

"Um, okay. So long as it's nothing serious. Why haven't you called Cindi?" Helen asked.

"I tried, but her phone isn't going through," he replied. He had wanted to tell her why he was arrested but, based on her reaction, he didn't want her to back off.

"Do you want me to let Cindi know what's happening when she comes back online?" Helen queried.

"Yes, I'd appreciate that. You can try in half an hour since I don't have access to my phone," Luke said.

"I can't make any promises because I'll be on a date, but I'll try," Helen said.

Luke frowned. "You'll be on a date? With who?"

"No offense, but that's none of your business, Luke," she said.

"We just got divorced. It's been less than a year," he said.

"There's no timetable for when one must move on. So if you're ready, you can do what I'm doing," Helen said.

"How long have you been seeing him?" Luke asked.

"Long enough," Helen replied. "I've got to go."

"Okay. Thanks for taking my call. Enjoy your... erm," Luke said, rubbing his temple. "Yeah, enjoy."

After he hung up, Luke stared at the phone. His jaw stiffened as he grit his teeth.

"Is everything okay?" Detective Tony asked.

"Yeah, everything will be fine," Luke replied. "That was my ex-wife. Things can be a little heavy with her."

Just then, Detective Shozi returned. She looked disappointed. "It checks out."

Detective Tony grunted and adjusted his belt. "Lucky you."

Luke smiled. "I told you I didn't do it. Can I go home now?"

"It's not proof of your innocence, but it's a first step. Yes, you can leave," Detective Tony said.

Luke stood up, energised. He strolled out of the room.

As he approached the front entrance, it surprised Luke to find Cindi waiting in the reception.

"I tried to call you a few minutes ago when I thought I would need to be bailed out," Luke said. "What's wrong with your phone?"

Cindi held it up. "It ran out of power, and nobody here seems to have one. Are you okay?"

"Yeah, I'm fine. Thanks for coming round. Let's go."

As they walked out, Cindi gave him an update.

"I just found out that Mark booked a one-way flight for yesterday to North Africa. It's a little strange, right?" Cindi said.

"He never took the flight for one obvious reason: he's dead. The question is: why did he book the flight, and why was it only one-way?" Luke asked.

"What are you trying to say?" she asked.

"He has money in the bank and runs a tight schedule. Why would he book a one-way ticket? People who do that don't intend to come back. Was he running from something, or someone? Did they get to him before he could get away?" Luke asked.

"You really think he was trying to disappear?" Cindi asked.

"I definitely want to disappear out of here on a one-way ticket right now. It's good to be out," Luke said with a tired smile. "Let's get something to eat, then figure out Mark's plan."

6

As Luke walked to the front door of Lynda's home, he felt a tinge of exhaustion. He'd hardly slept at the station, but he couldn't put off seeing her. He wondered how she was taking the news of Mark's death. She had hired him to find him, after all.

After he rang the doorbell, Lynda opened the door almost immediately, as if she'd heard him drive in.

Her hair was unkempt, and she wore no makeup. She'd also dressed down in trainers, and he guessed she hadn't left the house that day.

"Hey," Lynda said in a feeble voice.

"Hey. I thought I'd pass by and see you," Luke said.

"I heard they arrested you," Lynda said.

"Gossip travels fast. It was more like being taken in for questioning. Can I come in?" he said.

"Sure," she replied. He walked past her and down to the living room. She followed close behind. The place was neater than he expected it to be, although there was a shawl thrown over the couch and a few tear-drenched, crumpled pieces of tissue on the coffee table.

"Sorry, it's a bit of a mess," Lynda said as she gathered the tissues and threw them in a dustbin.

"It's understandable. How are you coping?" Luke asked.

She sighed. "Am I supposed to cope? I don't think anyone copes with this kind of thing. It breaks you in more ways than you can imagine. So frankly, I've got no idea how I'm doing."

Luke nodded. "Do you have friends and family coming over?"

"Yeah. My two sisters are coming later this evening. Mum is too far right now. Mark's brother was around this morning as we did the post-mortem," Lynda said. "You know, I sit here and I wish I hadn't taken that pottery class."

"Don't do that to yourself. There was no way you could've stopped it from happening," Luke replied.

"But I could. I could've gone with him to work. I've done before, I…" she didn't finish her statement as tears rolled down her cheeks. She grabbed some more tissue paper and dabbed her eyes. He watched in silence, giving her the time to compose herself. However, she started wheezing and holding her chest.

Luke rose quickly and went to her.

"What's wrong?" he asked.

She pointed to her throat. He knew she was struggling to breathe.

"Let's do some breathing exercises. Come on, work with me. Breath in…. and out," Luke instructed. He did this several times until she started breathing normally again.

"Lay on the couch," he said.

She followed his lead and lay on her back on the couch.

"You get that often?" Luke asked.

"When I'm overwhelmed by something. The doctor put

me on anxiety meds, but I don't like them. Sorry you had to deal with it all," she said.

"No problem. I'm glad I was around to help."

"I've been struggling to sleep and focus on things since Mark disappeared, and I guess it's all caught up with me now," Lynda said.

"Do you think George could've done this?" Luke asked.

"I can't tell, but I wouldn't be surprised," Lynda said. "But there were other strange messages as well."

Luke's eyes narrowed. "What do you mean by other strange messages?"

"We got small parcels and distinct threats on paper. Once, Mark's car was spray painted with a bull's-eye, as if he was a target," she said.

"Did you report this to the police?" Luke asked.

"No, I didn't. Mark didn't want us to," Lynda replied.

"Why is that?"

"He said he used to work with some high end clients who didn't want any publicity. He was avoiding headlines, which made little sense to me. To me, some of his VIP clients were a little shady," Lynda said.

Luke rubbed his chin. "Shady in what way?"

"You know, shady. Like people who deal in illegal stuff."

"Like drugs?" he asked.

She shrugged. "I wouldn't know."

Luke nodded. "Sorry about all this. I didn't want to ask you all these questions. I wanted to pass my condolences for your loss. If you need anything from me, just let me know. We can wrap things up after the funeral."

"Thanks for your kindness," Lynda said.

Luke rose to leave. "I'll be in touch to check in on things."

"You're going to find out who did this, right?" Lynda asked.

Luke smiled. "Our agreement was to just find Mark. We've done that."

"Yes, but this isn't how I wanted him to return home. They stole my peace and I want to know why. Can you help me?" she asked.

Luke paused for a second. "Sure. But I'll need to know more about your husband."

"What do you need?" she asked.

"I'd like to visit his offices. If possible, I'd like to check out the delivery manifest. What you said about the clients made me curious. There might be a clue in there about where he was going," Luke replied.

"Sure. I'll call them and tell them you're coming," Lynda replied.

"Thanks. If it's okay with you, I'll leave now," Luke said. "Stay safe and get some rest."

As he headed to his car, he felt sorry for her. Losing a loved one to such violence irked him, and he hoped to help her find answers.

Once inside his car, he called Cindi.

"Any updates on the hotel?" he asked.

"Yeah. The receptionist on duty that day says Mark arrived with the package, but he didn't leave it there. Instead, he was given another white envelope with a new destination," Cindi said.

Luke raised a brow. "Hold on. Had the receiver checked out of the hotel or something?"

"No, the receiver had never checked into the hotel. So this was like a stopover for Mark," Cindi said.

"Or a diversion by the receiver," Luke said.

"Maybe. They showed me the CCTV, and it matches

with what they told me about the whole thing," Cindi added.

"Who dropped off the envelope?" Luke asked.

"A courier wearing a bike helmet. They can't tell who it was, even from the CCTV footage. All we know is he wore a blue and white riding suit, with a matching helmet," Cindi said.

"So, no one knows what the note said?" Luke asked.

"Nope. Mark opened it and then left," Cindi said.

"Great. Thanks. Let's talk soon," Luke said.

He tapped his car's steering wheel a few times as he pondered what to do next. Had the receiver led Mark to his death, or were they just being cautious about a sensitive package?

7

———

THE NEXT MORNING, Luke drove to the Mach 1 offices. It was a chilly morning, and he found Freddie Vumisa, the manager, in his office wearing a heavier coat than necessary.

"I didn't think you'd be here this early, but I understand why," Freddie said. "She also told me the real reason you're here."

"Which is what?" Luke asked, narrowing his gaze.

"You're a security consultant who wants to find out what happened to her husband. It's such a terrible tragedy," Freddie said.

"It sure is. I just want to help in any way I can," Luke said. Inwardly, it amused him how Lynda smartly crafted his role in the unfolding investigation.

"Same here. She told me you wanted to see some documents. What do you need?" Freddie said.

"Could you share with me the records of the deliveries made in the past two months? I'd like to have a quick look," Luke said.

"Two months? That's a lot of business because we do

several deliveries in one day. It will take you longer than a quick look," Freddie said.

"That's fine with me. The more, the better," Luke replied.

"Okay. Wait here," Freddie said as he stood up. He walked out of the office.

About five minutes later, he returned with a large black book. He handed it to Luke, who scrolled through it. It was full of neatly done entries.

"That's got all our delivery clients for this year. You can narrow down to the two months you're interested in and then see how that helps streamline things," Freddie said.

"Thank you very much. Can I go through it here? It won't be long," Luke said.

"You're a speed reader?"

"Something like that," Luke replied.

"Very well. I'll be at the dispatch office in case you need me," Freddie said. With that, he turned and left, closing the door behind him.

Luke flipped through the book, eager to find something. He had developed into a fast reader these days, a necessary skill when confronted with limited time and access.

Most entries were in the clients' full names. However, several of the entries had initials only alongside a physical address for the drop off point. Luke knew these were the secret clients.

On the day he disappeared, the records showed Mark had two VIP deliveries scheduled: one to a certain B.N. at Melborough Drive, and the other to The Horse Trail Hotel. The parcel to the hotel had neither initials nor full name of the recipient. There was also nothing about the sender. None of the entries showed what was being ferried.

Once done, Luke tracked down Freddie and asked him

about the initials of the client Mark had gone to deliver to that day.

"I know that address," Freddie said. "He's this rich client called Barry Nelson, who lives in a lavish private estate in Melborough."

"You think he likes visitors?" Luke asked.

Freddie shrugged. "I wouldn't know."

"Well, let me find out and let you know," Luke replied.

Luke rushed to his car and drove out, heading to Melborough. It wasn't a distant suburb, but there was a traffic warning, so he took an alternative route to get there.

Soon, he was driving through tree-lined streets with manicured street hedges and people walking sausage dogs. Melborough had always been a rich man's paradise across South Africa's history.

The address brought him to a large black gate with a yellow rising barrier in front of it. A guard who wore tall boots, a dark blue uniform, beret and sunglasses walked up to the driver's window.

"How can I help you?" the guard asked.

"I'm here to see Mister Nelson," Luke said.

"Do you have an appointment?"

"No. But tell him it's about the special package delivered to him on the 4th," Luke said.

The guard's suspicious gaze lingered. He then walked back to the guardhouse. Through the slat windows, Luke watched as he called the main house. There was a brief exchange, and then the guard returned.

"He's ready to see you," the guard said.

"Thanks," Luke replied.

The guard raised the barrier and then pressed a button from the guardhouse. The large gate opened sideways, rolling at a steady pace to the right until it revealed the beautiful driveway ahead. He drove through the shaded driveway, which had very thick bushes and tall trees on each side.

The driveway soon revealed a large Gothic Revival-style country house. He could recognise the house's style through the clover shaped windows and pitched gables it had. His fascination with architecture had started when he moved into the motel after separating with his ex-wife. He'd been entertaining fantasies about building a new life if they never reconciled.

Upon knocking at the tall wooden front doors, a butler told him to wait in the hallway. Its hallway was impressive, with tall ceilings and delicate ornamental carvings done on the wooden beams lining the walls.

He heard the approaching footsteps of several men and saw them emerge round a corner in the hallway. Two muscular men in suits flanked a smartly dressed man.

"Hello there," Barry said in a smooth baritone drawl. Dressed in a fitting suit with no tie, his look was a blend between a serious boardroom heavy-hitter and a relaxed man. His manner of speaking sounded like an aristocrat who didn't mingle with people like Luke often, and if he did, it always had to benefit him first.

"Thank you for agreeing to meet me," Luke said. "I'm representing Mark from the Mach 1 delivery company."

"Where's Mark? He always comes alone," Barry said, his eyes darting around.

"That's true. Unfortunately, Mark is dead," Luke said.

Barry let out a whistle. "Are you serious? What happened?"

"He was murdered on the 4th," Luke said.

"That's sad to hear. Pass my condolences. I met him earlier that day," Barry said.

"I'll forward the kind words to his wife. So he delivered a parcel to you on that day?" Luke said.

"Yes, he delivered as always," Barry said.

"Do you mind telling me what was in the package?" Luke asked.

"No, I'm not telling you. It was a private package for a reason," Barry said.

"Fair enough," Luke said. He skipped to other minor questions and ten minutes later, he was back on the highway.

Barry's secretive nature made Luke want to investigate Mark's company operations more carefully. Was something else going on behind the scenes? How often had he served clients like Barry every week? He called Cindi, and she agreed to meet him for an evening coffee.

They met at what had now become one of their favourite meeting spots, Davies' restaurant. It had a simple ambience and menu and rarely got full. It was perfect for short business meetings. When he started the private investigator business, one of the restaurant booths had been their first office.

Because it was across town from Melborough, he found Cindi already waiting for him. It surprised him to see her already eating some chicken curry.

"I thought this was a coffee date?" Luke said.

Cindi shrugged. "I might as well make it dinner. It's been a long day."

Luke made his order for freshly brewed coffee, which was made from roasted Ethiopian coffee beans.

"Any update on the hotel delivery?" Luke asked.

Cindi shook her head. "Nothing more to add to what I had already told you."

Luke frowned. "It sounds like it was a treasure hunt or something."

"It does. It's strange how there's no record of it anywhere. This client wanted no written trace," Cindi said.

"Listen, I'm planning to go to the place where Lynda was taking her pottery classes to check her alibi. We can go as a couple," Luke said.

"Why as a couple?" Cindi asked.

"To blend in better," Luke replied.

"You're sure it's not because you're lonely?" Cindi asked.

"The only person I miss right now is Lily, my dog. I miss her terribly, but I have to do the once-a-week thing with my ex-wife," Luke said.

"Why don't you get another dog now that you're single?" Cindi said.

"I need to move out first, remember?" Luke said. "Maybe I won't get a dog. Maybe a new girlfriend is better."

Cindi chuckled again. "You need to get back to the dating scene first if you want a girlfriend. I can see that you're rusty."

They kept talking, witnessed a stunning sunset as the evening wore on, and then called it a night when darkness fell.

Early the next morning, they met at the office and left for the pottery class. It was an hour's drive away, and they enjoyed the gradual change as the high-rise buildings gave way to the open fields and grasslands. The scenery was therapeutic compared to the suffocating sights and sounds in city traffic, which he experienced every working day of the week.

They arrived at Arm of The Potter, a cottage bungalow located two kilometres off the main highway. The road leading to it was a well-conditioned murram road, so the ride was pleasant. Surrounding it were tall grasslands and a nearby maize farm.

A medium-sized man in his fifties with a puffy beard met them. He wore suspended jeans, a checked cotton shirt with rolled-up sleeves that revealed his hairy arms. His handshake was firm.

"Thank you for coming, I'm Wesley," the man introduced himself. "I own the place."

"I'm Richard, and this is my partner, Velona. A friend of ours recommended you to us and here we are," Luke said.

"That's great. Word of mouth works best for me. I've tried everything else, but you can't beat good old word-of-mouth advertising," a smiling Wesley said. "What were you looking for?"

"We just want to do new things together, and we felt pottery is something we can add to the list of activities we share," Luke said.

"I like it when couples do that. We have several in residence. By that I mean they come to attend classes here regularly. We have classes every Tuesday, Thursday, and Saturday afternoon from 2 p.m. Let me give you a tour of the place," Wesley said.

As he showed them the pottery space, the products he had made and the lay of the land, Luke was admiring the country life while doing some math.

"That was fun," Cindi later said as they leaned on the car, taking in the countryside view. They had completed the tour and were taking stock of their visit.

"Maybe I should move out here," Luke said. "It's relaxing and quiet."

"Can you afford it?" Cindi asked.

Luke shook his head. "One day. In the meantime, I have a theory. I don't think Lynda killed Mark. Like she said, she was here for the afternoon classes starting at 2 p.m. This means we're looking at another suspect."

"Who?" Cindi asked.

"My hunch is that George, the disgruntled employee, knows something," Luke said with finality.

8

———————

THE NEXT DAY, Luke drove up to George's house and he could hear loud music coming from inside. It was a lower middle-class neighbourhood, with identical houses lining both sides of the street. The front doors and parking spaces faced each other. Luke parked right next to the beaten up sedan that was parked outside the house. The dilapidated car was a testament to George's struggles after being fired, Luke mused.

There were two empty oil drums in front of George's house, which seemed out of place to Luke. He knocked on the front door three times with no response. All he could hear was the loud music.

He got in, anyway. His foot hit a pile of carton boxes the moment he stepped in. He quickly realised the corridor was cluttered with boxes. He skipped them and got to the living room. There, he saw an overweight, barefoot man in a vest and pants dancing. It wasn't great dancing in Luke's view, but the man seemed to be lost in his movements.

"Hello!" Luke shouted. George didn't hear him. Luke looked for the sound system and switched it off.

George froze, startled. "Who are you?"

"Hello, George. Relax, I'm here on behalf of Mach 1. Can we talk?" Luke said.

"You interrupted my session. What do you want?" George asked.

"To talk to you. You've wanted to talk to someone from Mach 1 for ages. Well, here's your chance," Luke said.

"What's your name and who are you at Mach 1?" George queried.

"My name is Luke Mbeki. I'm here on behalf of the company."

"That doesn't answer my question. I've never heard of you. What do you do?" George insisted.

"George, you've not been at the company for close to two years. You surely can't know everybody, can you? Sit down and let's talk," Luke said.

George hesitated, then sat on the arm of his chair.

"What do you want to talk about?" George asked.

"You were let go some time back after an issue with the boss. I know you've been in touch in different ways. Why haven't you moved on?" Luke asked.

"Moved on to what? They haven't paid my dues after an unfair dismissal," George said.

"Did you report it to the labour union or take it to court?"

George scoffed. "I don't need to jump through hoops to get what's owed to me."

"Are you still unhappy about things? Because, from the way you're dancing, you seem happier," Luke said.

"I'm simply celebrating freedom. I'm still free to do that, right?" George replied.

"What's freedom exactly?"

"Freedom means justice. I'm celebrating that," George replied.

"I'm sure that you know by now what happened to Mark," Luke said.

"Karma did its job. I didn't have to do much," George said.

"You're saying you had nothing to do with it?" Luke asked.

George smiled. "Nothing. I let it all go."

"Okay. Where were you on the 4th, the day Mark died?" Luke queried.

George scratched the back of his neck. "I was at home."

"Were you alone or with someone?"

"Do I look like I live with someone?" George said.

"You've got to prove your whereabouts, you know," Luke said.

George narrowed his eyes. "What do you do again? Because you're asking strange questions."

"I work in security, and we've been receiving the letters you've been sending Mark. Why have you been doing that?" Luke asked.

"Because he wasn't listening. If he listened to me, bad luck wouldn't have found him," George said.

"You think this was bad luck, someone shooting him to death?" Luke asked.

"Like I said, karma did its job," George replied.

"Did you enjoy working at Mach 1?" Luke asked.

George grinned. "Are you kidding? It was one of the best jobs ever. I'd worked at one other place previously and they had shut down after messing up the business. Mark came in at the right time and helped me save myself because I was a wreck."

Luke nodded slowly. "So, he gave you a second chance?"

"Something like that. I think Mach 1 is the reason I'm alive today. I was rash and stupid back then. When Mark fired me, I lost something," George said.

Luke concluded that George's self-worth and identity were tied to the company. He had nothing else going on outside his work-life, which was an unhealthy union.

"How was Mark as a boss?" Luke asked.

George sighed and stared at the ceiling for a moment.

"At first, we got along really well. For the first few years, things were good. He was a genial man, and I looked up at him as a mentor of sorts. He had a brilliant business mind. Actually, I can safely say he's the smartest man I've ever met. No offense," George said.

Luke raised a brow. "Why would I be offended?"

"I don't know. People think of themselves in different ways. Anyway, I watched him grow the company year after year and it was a great experience. When I get the capital to start a business, I'll follow his example," George said.

"What was it about the way he did things that impressed you?"

"The way he built his teams. Everyone wanted to fight for him, even when he'd ask for crazy things. Five o'clock would get there and you'd want to give him overtime, which he didn't pay for, of course. We were a small and efficient team of focused individuals," George said.

"Then what changed?" Luke asked.

George bit his lower lip. "I'm not sure. I used to think he got worse. Now I realise he was that way all along. I just opened my eyes. I found out Mark was a cold, calculating man who ruined lives."

"That's a bold statement to make without giving proof. What did you see that made you think that?" Luke prodded.

"He started being controlling when the VIP thing started. It was bringing in more cash than the regular clients. I mean, you could do two VIP deliveries and make more cash than ten regular deliveries. So he got very touchy with those. If you messed up, he'd throw a fit and tear you down in public, which I found unnecessary. I told him this, and he'd change for a week, then go back to his old ways. He introduced new rules as we rebranded. The place became less carefree and more about the rule of law. His way or the highway. It lost its soul," George said.

"Did he fire you for standing up to him?" Luke asked.

"I know he did. He was just waiting to use the delivery mistake to get me out of there. I mean, other people had messed up deliveries and were still on the job. Why was I fired for losing a parcel to thugs?" George said.

"You were robbed while on a job? How?" Luke asked.

"Well, it seems silly when I think about it. I wasn't carjacked or anything. I hadn't eaten the whole day, so I stopped over at a convenience store to get a takeaway bite. The five minutes there was enough for someone to get into the car and steal the package from the back seat," George said.

"Did you check the CCTV or something?"

"It wasn't working. Eyewitnesses said they saw a white hatchback leaving, but no one told me the make or the number plate. The stuff was gone. When I told Mark, he had a huge fit and fired me," George said. "I reached out to him, apologised and told him about my personal situation, but he didn't care. He didn't even give me benefits, saying it was compensation for the lost business."

"This made you angry," Luke said.

"Of course. I helped him build that business. I used my contacts in the business to set him up. Some of the staff he has there to this day were brought in by me. In another world, he'd have given me a stake in the company," George said.

"Fair enough. But let's cut to the chase. In your anger, you've sent him a lot of messages and followed him to places you shouldn't have been to," Luke said.

"I was trying to make peace," George said.

"By sending threats?" Luke asked.

"He wouldn't listen to me when I was polite. I had to get creative," George said.

"Creative enough to kidnap him and kill him?" Luke asked.

"I didn't kill him," George replied.

"Stop the games, George. Someone did. Someone who knew how he drives, where he goes to, and knew exactly where and when to strike. You knew his patterns after working with him for so long. You were angry at him for firing you. Did you push it too far?" Luke prodded.

"I didn't do it. If I did it, it would've been a big splash. I would've wanted the world to know. To shame him the way he did to me. I wouldn't have done it quietly, that's for sure," George said. As he rose to his feet. "You need to talk to his ex- girlfriend, Faith. Or his mistress Queen."

Luke's eyes widened. "What mistress?"

George chuckled. "Oh. You haven't heard about Queen? You should look her up. I'm just a guy and I'm going to the washroom."

"Wait. How do you know about her?" Luke asked.

George kept walking without responding. Luke sighed. He hoped George was making up things. Luke stood as well, adrenaline rippling through his system. He paced around the living room, then spotted a door that was masked by a tall bookshelf. He went to it, paused as he looked over his shoulder, and turned the door handle. The door opened in silence and he was inside.

It was dark, and he flicked the switch. It was a tiny room, possibly a modification, with a desk, chair, and an old desktop computer. But what stood out was the noticeboard above the desk. It was on the wall facing him. It had newspaper cuttings, coloured notes and photographs of several people. Luke went closer and he could see articles about the Mach 1 business. His eyes were drawn to the pictures of Mark and Lynda. They both had bulls' eyes drawn in red felt pen around their heads.

9

A SHOCKED LUKE went back into the living room and sat in the same spot he was when George left. Minutes later, George returned.

"You're still here?" George asked.

"It would be rude to just leave," Luke said.

"You technically broke into my house, so it doesn't matter," George said.

"No, my mother raised me differently. I asked a question as you left about Queen," Luke said.

"I'm not answering anything," George said.

"Then at least give me her address if you have nothing to hide," Luke said.

George pursed his lips, then went to a work desk tucked in the corner. He scribbled something on a piece of paper and handed it to Luke.

"Velum Apartments. Don't ask me how I know," George said.

Luke glanced at the paper and pocketed it. He got to his feet.

"Thanks. I hope you'll ease up on the letters now?" Luke said.

George grinned. "It's a good day today. Tomorrow is unknown. Please don't come here again."

Luke left and debated with himself whether to go to Mama Ash's dog sanctuary, which he always did when he wanted to think. After their separation, Helen had maintained custody of Lily, their brown-furred Golden Retriever. Volunteering at the dog shelter helped him organise his thoughts better, and he needed to digest the chaos he had seen at George's house.

However, he also needed to make a choice. He opted to meet Cindi instead and talk it through.

"Should we report this guy to the police or wait?" Luke asked Cindi as they sat in his car parked in a street next to Cedar Mall.

"You believe he killed him, don't you?" Cindi asked.

"Yes, I do. Although I have seen no tangible evidence. But the threats are a pattern, and the wall proves motive. Surely, they should have questioned him by now, but I doubt they have," Luke said.

Cindi drummed her fingers on the purse she'd placed on her lap.

"You should wait. Maybe we should watch him. If you found him celebrating, then he might make another mistake," Cindi said.

"You're suggesting a stake out? You realise that will kill any hopes of me building a social life?" Luke said.

Cindi laughed. "I'll download for you a dating app. That should help you connect with some women as you wait for something to happen."

"Those things work?" Luke asked.

"Mostly, you can have a little fun on a date. But if you're

looking for a wife, you might need to do extra leg work," Cindi said.

"I wonder if Mark used those dating apps to meet his mistress," Luke said.

"Ask her when you meet her," Cindi said. "I've got to head out. You'll be fine, right?"

"I'll try to be. Thanks," Luke said.

Cindi got out of the car and walked away. Luke went into Cedar Mall to buy some snacks for the stakeout.

Later, Luke drove to George's house and parked several car lengths away from George's car which was parked outside his house. He ate the sandwiches he'd bought with some yoghurt. He then eased down in the driver's seat.

As he watched the street, he considered George's disposition. He was living alone, buried in his own imaginations of what life should be like. He hadn't recovered from getting fired, and in his bitterness, had started a campaign to bring down Mark and his business. Would he want to kill?

It would be gradual, but possible. The wall with photos signalled a growing obsession that could get dangerous. Luke guessed that if he searched George's computer, he'd find interesting search results about guns and murder. He probably binged crime shows on television.

In a strange way, Luke could see a similarity in his life with George's situation. They had both lost their dream jobs and needed to start anew. They both lived alone in lesser circumstances than they wanted. The only difference was that Luke had a support system and the private investigation business was working. What if he had neither? He'd lose himself, much like George had.

Luke saw George step out of his house. He wore slacks, a jumper and a cap, as casual as can be. He got into his car and drove off. By this time, Luke had straightened up and started his car engine. He followed some distance behind. The sun shone into the car and he lowered the sun visor while hoping the windshield tint kept him anonymous in case George used his rear-view mirror.

George drove at a leisurely pace, which was good enough for Luke. It helped him hang back and blend in with the rest of the traffic. If he was following someone driving fast, he ran more risk of being noticed. Luke would allow another car to come between them occasionally to avert suspicion.

After a fifteen-minute drive, George stopped outside the post office. Luke drove past him and parked. He watched him walk into the building and was tempted to follow, but it made little sense. If he was meeting someone, which Luke highly doubted, then he'd have taken the risk. Five minutes later, George emerged with letters in hand. He got into his car and drove off. Luke let him pass, then followed.

George drove as if he was heading back home, then branched left. He drove to the neighbourhood supermarket. Luke parked across from him so that he maintained his line of sight and waited.

It was half an hour later when George emerged. Luke expected him to be pushing out a trolley, but all he had was a small shopping bag. He drove out and Luke kept trailing him. This time, George drove towards the museum area and entered the museum's park, which was open to the public.

It was a recreational park like any other, with indigenous trees, walkways, small ponds and picnic areas. What made it unique was it had the statues of national heroes like Steve Biko at certain locations.

Was George looking for some fresh air to clear his thoughts? Was he going for a workout? Luke took out his cap and let it hang low over his eyes to mask his identity, then got out to follow him on foot.

They walked for a few metres. George still carried his bag, but he didn't look like he was there for a workout. There were other people at the park, some with dogs, others jogging, and couples taking a romantic stroll.

After the short walk, George stopped at a park bench. He sat down. Luke put on his earphones and went to stand next to a small pond. He wished he had some bird food to throw at the ducks in the pond, but he opted to play the role of a man lost in his thoughts. He had a good line of sight to George, who was oblivious to his presence.

George reached into the shopping bag and took out a bag of potato crisps. He started eating them as he looked around. This went on for close to twenty minutes. To Luke, this stake out was becoming boring now. He'd hoped there would be something that George would do to spark his suspicion, but he'd just confirmed that he was a lonely man without a social life.

Luke was about to leave after standing next to the pond became too awkward when he saw another man sit at the other end of George's bench. Luke lingered, hoping to see how George would react. Would he stand up and leave, finding another bench for himself? It would be a sign of how much he'd been cutting himself off from society.

However, the opposite happened. Luke didn't catch it at first, but the two men were talking to each other without exchanging eye contact. George would say something, and the man would respond. The new arrival wore a long coat which harboured a suit underneath and black shoes, as if he'd just come from the office.

The man reached inside his coat, took out a thick brown envelope and slid it towards George. George glanced at it, took it, and peeked inside. He looked to be counting cash notes. George nodded, muttered something. The man in the coat then nodded. They then stopped talking to each other for a few minutes as if nothing had happened.

George put the envelope in the bag he had carried and went on eating the crisps until the bag was empty. He then rose and walked back to his car. Luke wanted to follow George, then changed his mind. He stayed on, watching the man on the bench. Ten minutes later, the man rose and Luke trailed behind him. As he did this, Luke could only think of one thing: was George a hit man?

10

———————

THE MAN WALKED BACK to the same car park where Luke had parked, got into his SUV, and drove off. Luke scampered to his car and sped out of the parking, keen to catch up. Fortunately, they encountered a traffic jam leading up to an intersection, and he could make ground.

He opted to follow the stranger instead of George because he knew how to find George. This other guy needed to be identified properly. The traffic jam cleared, and he kept trailing him.

Eventually they arrived at a shopping centre in the eastern part of the city, and the man parked his car in a designated parking spot. Luke parked several parking spots away and got out of the car. He walked casually towards the building. When he saw that the man was yet to exit his car, Luke pretended to be tying his shoes laces. Eventually, the man got out of his car and entered the building. Luke followed closely. Instead of taking the lifts, the man took the stairs. Luke kept up, keen not to look too eager.

They arrived on the second floor and the man walked

through an open door and into an office. A sign above the door read: *psychiatrist's office.*

The man walked straight past the reception and Luke figured he worked there. Luke lingered for about five minutes before walking to the reception desk. A middle-aged woman smiled up at him.

"Hello, how may I help you?" the receptionist asked.

"Hi. I've been dealing with some stuff after separating with my wife. I wanted someone to talk to," Luke said.

"We're glad you've come over. Is this your first time here?" she asked.

"Yes, it is. Do you have something I can read about the place? I'd like to book a session, if possible," Luke replied.

The receptionist reached for something in a drawer and handed him a pamphlet.

"That's our brochure. You can sit down and read it. Once you're comfortable, we can book a session for you," the receptionist said.

Luke sat on one of the four waiting chairs and went through the pamphlet. He wasn't interested in the rates. All he wanted was the name of the man, and he found it. His portrait photo, along with his name and credentials, were in the brochure. He was Doctor Walter Wendosi, a psychiatrist with over twenty years' experience having studied at South African and Australian universities.

Satisfied, Luke went back to the reception.

"Let me take it home and give it some thought. Maybe I need to talk to my estranged wife and see if she wants to work on this with me or not," Luke said.

The receptionist smiled. "Of course, I understand. It's also a good thing you want to include her. Few men do that."

When he got back to the car, Luke called Cindi and

asked her to find out more about the doctor. Afterwards, he spent some time reading the brochure. An hour later, he stepped out to take a walk in the shopping centre, always ensuring he could see the doctor's car at all times.

With stake outs, Luke had initially hated them. He disliked being far from the comfort of a warm bed as he observed a person of interest. Sitting in the car would get cold if the weather was chilly, and he'd avoid putting on the heat most of the time. In addition, he'd struggle to choose what to eat. He didn't eat bread anymore and French fries were out of the question. He'd often settle for some biltong, a tasty beef jerky, and a mug of steaming coffee or tea.

Tonight, as he waited outside Doctor Walter Wendosi's office, he was better prepared. He'd got some fried cassava chips, which he found tasty, and some biltong stew from a new restaurant. He downed the meal with a mug of tea.

Darkness fell. If Walter had stayed in his office for a late working night, Luke knew he'd have dozed off, as he was well fed and sleepy. But when Walter sauntered out of his office and to his car, the drowsiness disappeared. Luke watched Walter get into his car and drive off.

Luke followed him and was quickly reminded that it would be tricky to keep up with the doctor's SUV, which was more powerful. He came up with a plan; he'd drive as fast as he could in the open streets, where he'd be left in the dust, and catch up with him at the intersections.

This worked, and he was soon coming to a stop some metres away from Walter's home. By the time he turned his engine off, Walter was hugging his wife at the front door. Two kids, possibly five and ten years old, also came out to embrace him. They entered the house, and the street was silent again. Luke was in an upper middle-class neighbourhood with identical homes on each side. No one was walking out at night, and the silence was broken by leaves rustling in the trees.

Luke sat in the car for a few moments until one of the street-facing windows in Walter's house came on. Luke could see some movement in the room, but he was at a poor angle to tell what was really happening. So he opted to go for a stroll.

He got out of the car and looked around him. There was no one walking along the street. He started strolling down the paved sidewalk and could soon see clearly across the street into Walter's house. Walter and his family were setting the table for dinner. Luke couldn't tell what meal it was, but judging from the number of bowls, it was a splendid feast.

Watching them laugh and share stories as they ate made him feel a tinge of sadness. He missed his wife, and the dream they had of starting a family. They never got pregnant, and this troubled him, even after their separation. Maybe if they had a child earlier, they would still be together. Although his mother had always told him that children don't fix a marriage, he felt that in his and Helen's case, it's what they needed most.

He strolled up and down the same stretch of sidewalk for four more laps before he returned to his car. He got in and felt slightly warmer since he'd left the car heater on. As he sat in the driver's seat, he decided there was no longer any need to watch the doctor.

He took out his phone and dialled Helen's number. Instead of her picking the call, someone else did.

"Hello, Helen's phone," a deep masculine voice said.

The voice jarred Luke, and he adjusted his seating position. "Hello, I'd like to speak to Helen," Luke said.

"Helen is out for the moment, but you can leave a message if you like," the man replied.

Luke rubbed his temple. "What is she doing out at this hour?"

"Who are you to be asking that?" the man asked.

"Her ex-husband," Luke said.

"Oh, you're her ex? My bad," the man said in a near jovial fashion. "Well, I think she's moved on, so you don't have to wonder what she's doing at this hour. Do you have a message you'd like me to give her?"

Luke clenched his free hand around the steering wheel. "I'm glad she's moved on. Just tell her I'll call her tomorrow about the dog," Luke replied.

"Sure thing. Goodnight," the man said.

Luke didn't respond. He ended the call and shook his head. That was a dumb thing to do. He looked at his phone again and searched for Sally's number. She was the restaurant server. He called her.

"Who is this?" Sally asked in a silky voice.

"This is Luke. You recommended the fried cassava chips to me?" Luke said.

"Oh, hey! I thought you'd never call," she said.

"Well, here I am now. I was wondering if...," Luke said, thinking of where to take her. "...if you'd like to have some coffee, sometime? Maybe the day after tomorrow at the restaurant in the Jefferson hotel?"

"Yeah, sure. How about we make it a breakfast date?" she asked.

"Sure, let's do that. Say 7?" Luke suggested.

"Make it 8.30. I'm not exactly a morning person," she said.

"That's too late for me. 7.30 is my last offer," Luke said.

"Okay, I'll do 7.30. I'll make it work," Sally replied.

"Are you sure?"

"Yeah, I'm sure. Trust me. See you then!" Sally replied.

"See you," Luke said.

As he hung up, he had a feeling she'd let him down, but he didn't know how.

He'd just switched on his car when the phone rang. It was Detective Shozi. Luke hesitated, wondering why she was calling him at that hour. In fact, only Detective Tony called him. This was the first time his partner was doing this.

"Hello, detective," Luke said.

"Hello, Luke. Sorry to call you so late. Where are you?"

"Heading home," Luke said, keen not to give away his whereabouts.

"Are you sure?"

"Yes."

"Okay. I'll need you to report to the police station tomorrow morning," Detective Shozi said.

Luke frowned. "Why?"

"You'll know tomorrow. Just make sure you come in," Detective Shozi said.

As Luke hung up, he felt the goose bumps spread all over his body. *What did she know that involved him?*

11

Luke was at the police station by eight the next morning. He wanted to get that out of the way first so that he could go on with the rest of his day. He hoped to find Detective Shozi present, but he had to wait for another half an hour before she arrived.

"Good for you to come in early," Detective Shozi said as they walked into her office.

"What's going on that you couldn't share on the phone?" Luke asked.

"You'll see soon enough. Sit and give me ten minutes," Detective Shozi said. She took off her coat, draped it over her chair, and left.

Luke eased into one of the visitor chairs and scanned the office. It was unglamorous, with steel file cabinets that had seen better days, an old office desk stacked with files, and worn out seats. He believed that if the police were able to solve cases most of the time, then the office furniture wouldn't matter. But in this case, the police were stretched thin, and it showed. Sitting there didn't inspire confidence.

"Come with me," Detective Shozi said, startling Luke.

Luke shot out of the seat and followed the detective down the corridor. They walked down a second corridor and went past two security checks. Detective Shozi had to use a special card pass to gain access. They were going further into the lower levels of the police station when they came to the third door. It had a sticker printed: 'Ballistic test'.

Detective Shozi ushered Luke into an indoor shooting range. On their end stood booths where you could prepare your firearm before firing it. At the far end of the room were round and human-form shooting targets punched with holes.

"You're going to need these," Detective Shozi said, handing him a set of protective headphones.

"What for?" Luke asked.

"I need you to help me test the rare pistol from the crime scene. I want to know how it fires," the detective said.

Luke's eyes widened. "I've never fired a gun before."

Detective Shozi smiled. "Let's see what you can do, anyway."

"But you could've done it without me, right?" Luke asked. "Professionals do these things, right?"

"Yes, but why not kill two birds with one stone? Look at it this way: it strengthens your case, since you weren't there," the detective replied.

It still made little sense to Luke, but he felt he couldn't back out now. He put on the headphones and waited. Detective Shozi put on a pair of gloves, then took out the gun from the evidence bag.

"Here you go," she said, holding it out to him.

"I need gloves too," he said.

"No, you don't. You're simply going to fire it," she said.

"With all due respect, detective. You're asking me to fire a gun, used in a murder, without gloves. I'll have my finger-prints on the gun and gunpowder residue on my hands. That's not a good thing for my case, is it? I'm not doing it without gloves," he said.

"You're being paranoid. I'm not setting you up. Why would I do that in a police station?" she asked.

"I'm wondering the same thing. If it's just a test, then you shouldn't have a problem with me wearing gloves," he said.

They exchanged steely looks, then the detective offered him gloves. He quickly put them on, then took the gun.

"All you have to do is point and shoot one target on the other side," the detective said.

Luke felt the cold barrel in his hands. The gun was lighter than he expected, and his index finger fit the trigger nicely. He almost dropped it as he lost balance, prompting Detective Shozi to admonish him. However, she didn't offer to show him the right way to hold it. He held it up the way he'd seen it being done in police shows and pointed at one of the round targets. He could feel Detective Shozi's eyes on his back, watching his every move.

He pressed the trigger, and nothing happened. He pressed it two more times. All he could hear was a metallic click.

"There are no bullets in the chamber," he said.

"Just keep holding it up," the detective said.

He turned to look at her and saw her holding a tape measure and another device that looked like a mini-telescope.

"Keep still as you hold the gun," she said. Using the mini-telescope, she looked through it over his shoulder and jotted down something in a notebook.

"What are you doing?" he asked.

"Taking notes. That doesn't bother you, does it?" she asked.

She walked up to him. With the tape measure, she measured the length of his outstretched arm from his shoulder and followed it up by measuring the height of the gun from the floor. She jotted down these numbers, too.

"There you go. Hand me back the gun, please," Detective Shozi said.

Luke gave the gun back and took off the gloves. "That's it?"

"That's it," she replied without looking at him.

When they returned to her office, they found Detective Tony seated at the desk.

"How was it down there?" Detective Tony asked.

Luke raised a brow but didn't respond. He thought Detective Shozi was acting on her own, showing her dislike for him. But with Detective Tony in the know, Luke kept his cool.

"It was pretty good. I took the measurements they asked for. Sending them in, so I'll leave you guys to it," Detective Shozi said. She grabbed her coat from the chair and left.

"Sorry about the short notice, but we're trying to close this case as soon as possible," Detective Tony said.

"But you didn't need to call me in," Luke said.

"We're just putting you out of the equation of suspects. It's a good thing," the detective replied.

"What other reports do you have about the gun?" Luke asked.

Detective Tony leaned forward. "Well, we know it's a rare gun and has been fired twice recently. We're trying to trace its origins and we've got a few good leads."

"Am I still a suspect?" Luke asked.

"You're already low on our list. This might get you over the line," Detective Tony said.

"That's not reassuring," Luke said.

"I'd rather be real with you than not," Detective Tony replied.

"Can I leave now?" Luke asked.

"Sure. I'll be in touch in case of any developments," the detective said.

Luke said an uneasy goodbye and left. He walked out of the police station with a hasty gait, wanting to get as far away from the place as possible. He had so many questions on his mind. Why had they called him in, yet he had an alibi? Why were they insisting that he test the gun without gloves? Was a case against him being put together, although he wasn't there during the murder and didn't even know how to fire a gun?

Part of him felt he had acquitted himself by his truthful performance of mishandling the gun, but he still had doubts about their intentions. Detective Tony was a straight and honest investigator, but even the best of us behave differently when under pressure. Were his bosses pushing him to make an arrest?

Luke needed to clear his head. He drove to Mama Ash's Dog Shelter. It had been too long since he last visited.

When he walked into the sanctuary, he found Mambatho, the place's manager, in the pets' operating room. It was a much simpler and accessible space than the regular one. Mambatho was attending to a German Shepherd with an injured foot, helped by her veterinary assistant, Freda. Luke noticed the dog was unconscious under an anaesthetic.

"You should put on an overcoat if you're going to be in here," Mambatho remarked.

"Is that the best way to say you miss me?" Luke asked. "I'm not getting a hug today?"

"Not while I'm attending to a patient," she said.

They both laughed.

"Can I help?" he asked.

"Not until you clear that frown from your face," Mambatho said.

"What frown?" Luke said.

"You can hide it when you laugh, but not when you go quiet. What's wrong?" Mambatho asked.

"Nothing's wrong," he said.

"I told you a long time ago, because I work with animals which can't speak, I've developed a strong sixth sense. That way, I can tell when they're distressed. You, my friend, aren't a dog, but you're definitely distressed about something," Mambatho said.

Luke sighed. "I've had a crazy start to the day, that's all. I came here to see if I can relax a little."

"That won't work. I told you that these dogs have seen a lot of distress already. You should only come here when you're in a better place. You'll rub off that distress on them," Mambatho said.

"What do you want me to do?"

"Take a break, regroup, come back when you're relaxed and ready to show some love again," Luke said.

"That's what I want to do right now," Luke protested.

"You can't offer what you have in small quantities. Go push off those frustrations, then your chest will be free and shoulders lighter," Mambatho said.

Luke thought about it and had to concede.

"You know what? You're right. I'll take your advice and I'll be back here before long," Luke said.

"I hope so," Mambatho said with a smile.

He left and called Kabelo and Cindi. They were at the Davies' restaurant.

He drove straight there. He needed some liveliness around him to break his depressing train of thought. If he needed a pick me up, they were his only back up option. By the time he arrived, it was late afternoon, and they were sipping coffee with some rusk biscuits.

After Luke had narrated to them the day's events, Cindi smiled.

"Should we take you to the movies to unwind?" she asked.

"You're sure he doesn't need an exorcism? Someone's looking at him with an evil eye," Kabelo said with a laugh.

"It's not that serious, guys," Luke said.

"But seriously, Luke. When was the last time you had fun? Or went out on a date?" Cindi asked.

"I can't recall," Luke said. "That's not a good look."

"You bet it's not," Cindi said. "You need balance in your life."

"He needs to go to the gym, and then afterwards find a woman or two to charm," Kabelo said.

"Just one is enough," Cindi said.

"But to get one, he must explore options. Not everyone is the same," Kabelo said.

"I can agree about the gym bit. The other stuff he has to figure out for himself. Luke, where do you meet your women?" Cindi asked.

"I don't meet any women. You know this, right?" Luke said.

"Did you try the app I told you about?" Cindi said.

"I didn't need to. I already got a date for tomorrow morning," Luke said.

"I don't believe you. From where?"

"I met her at a restaurant I checked out," Luke replied.

"Well, one date isn't enough. Give me your phone," Cindi said.

"Don't do it, brother. Don't give a woman your phone," Kabelo said.

"Stay out of this, Kabs. Pass me your phone," Cindi insisted.

Luke chuckled and handed her his phone. She fiddled around with it for a few minutes, then gave it back.

"There's an application I downloaded for you and opened an account already. Luke 2020," Cindi said.

"You downloaded a dating app?" Luke asked.

"I'm only helping you. Now, just wait for the messages to roll in. You'll be fine," she said.

"Does this thing work?" Luke asked Kabelo.

"*Eish*, you forget I'm married with kids, right? I don't need those things," Kabelo said.

Luke studied the home screen of the Love Pear App. Connected to one of his social media accounts, it already had one of his better profile photos on it, plus a short blurb that Cindi had written to introduce him.

A man who knows how to find buried treasure.

"I don't like the intro," he said.

"Why don't you wait and see if it works," Cindi said.

"Speaking of treasure, Kabs I need your help with something. It's about the small pistol they found at the crime scene. I need to know where it came from before the police do. Can you spread the word on the streets that I'm looking for it?" Luke asked.

"I'll need to be careful with that one. Once a gun is hot, then anything you ask about it might get to the police. We don't want that," Kabelo said. "Give me some time, I'll ask quietly, and let's see what comes up. Why are you looking for that info?"

"I want to find Mark's killer," Luke said. "I also don't want the police to use it against me. If they're trying to frame me, I have to stay ahead of the game."

12

As Luke stared across the table at his date, he wondered why he was subjecting himself to torture so early in the morning. They sat in a hotel restaurant with one of the best breakfast courses he could find. Sprawled before them was a hearty meal, courtesy of the buffet offering: bacon, Spanish omelette, boerewors sausages, toasted bread, fruit salad and mugs of tea. It was a feast that he was enjoying, but his date couldn't stop talking.

"So when we went out last night, we meet Kuzi Bones. He has the best *amapiano*, simply the best mix of mid to high tempo South African house music to get you dancing. I couldn't believe it. We ended up leaving the place at four in the morning," Sally said as she held up a sausage with a fork. In her early twenties, she had a cheery personality.

"At four? Is this why you're not a morning person?" Luke asked.

Sally giggled. "It's one reason. But I sometimes just sleep late when I don't go out."

"How often do you go out?" he said.

"Maybe four or five times a week. There's a show or

performer somewhere every day of the week. And since I love dancing, I've got to be there," she replied.

Luke almost choked on his toast. He took a sip of tea to clear his airway.

"You go out every day? How do you focus on your work at the restaurant during the day?" he asked.

"My shift starts from eleven to evening, and I'm always on my feet, so it's easy. It doesn't hurt to go out, you know. I want to be an events manager next, so this is my preparation," Sally said.

Luke nodded. He believed she loved the nightlife more than her career aspirations. He couldn't relate to what she was saying, as the last time he went out was when Victor, his former business partner, was still alive.

"Tell me something about you that has nothing to do with music and partying," he said.

Sally laughed until her eyes got teary. Luke sat there, bemused.

"Frankly, that's my whole life. I know some people find it weird, but I call it commitment," Sally said.

Luke sighed, because he knew he couldn't take it anymore. He called the water and asked for his food to be packed.

"You're leaving?" Sally asked in surprise.

Luke leaned forward. "Let me be straight with you. We live in two different worlds that won't meet. I don't think I can do this. But thanks for making the time."

"Can I at least get a burger before you leave? For lunch," she asked.

Luke turned down her request and left. He was gracious, but didn't like greed.

As he was getting into the car, his phone rang. It was Kabelo.

"Boss, are you somewhere we can talk?" Kabelo asked.

"Yeah, go ahead," Luke replied.

"I found the shop that sold the gun. It's on Fifth Avenue in Wempa. Are you able to come over or you'd like me to check it out alone?"

"That was fast. Wait for me, I'll be there in an hour if traffic allows," Luke said, his mind already conjuring a route across the city. Wempa was in a middle-income area of the city, but the traffic always made the half-hour trip longer.

"Sharp. I'll wait for you, but I'm a little hungry, so I'll go have some lunch here," Kabelo said.

"Dig in and I'll refund you," Luke said.

The drive to Wempa took forty-five minutes. It was an area full of high-rise residential buildings. Most of the residents were local, but there had been a large influx of residents from other Africa nations that had settled there in recent years. It was testament to their hardworking drive when they trooped to the city centre and industrial zones every morning and returned every evening.

He found Kabelo waiting for him at the corner of Fifth Street.

"You're full, I hope?" Luke asked.

"Yeah, I'm good," Kabelo replied.

Luke handed him some cash to reimburse his lunch bill.

"It's that shop over there, Desa Pawnshop. It's not that busy during the day from what I've seen, but I'm told at night it comes alive. Most people don't want to be seen around a pawn shop. Human pride," Kabelo said.

"Understandable. How did you get the lead so fast?" Luke asked.

Kabelo chuckled. "If I tell you, that wouldn't be right. I've got my ears to the street. I protect my network, so don't worry about it. Ready to go?"

"Yeah," Luke said. "You want to shoot this straight or role play?"

"Shoot it straight. No point of beating around the bush in these parts," Kabelo advised.

They walked to the pawnshop and entered. Although it was the first time for Luke in a pawnshop, he found it cramped. There were glass displays on each side leading up to the counter. Behind the counter stood two people of Indian descent, a middle-aged woman and an older gentleman.

"Good afternoon to you," Luke said.

"Good afternoon," the lady said. "How may we help you?"

"We're looking for a rare item. A gun," Luke said.

"We rarely sell guns, so it depends on which one you want," the lady replied with a smile.

"It's a small pistol around this big, and it has a gold-plated surface. Have you seen it?" Luke asked.

The lady and the man glanced at each other. They spoke in whispered Hindi, then the lady turned back to him.

"Are you looking to buy one or to find out who bought the one we had?" the lady asked.

"The latter," Luke replied.

"Well, we sold it to a lady some weeks ago. On the four-teenth of May. She had brunette hair, looked around thirty years old," the woman said.

"You're sure it was a brunette?" Luke asked.

"Yes, because I remember little else after that," the lady replied. "She paid cash, no names on the receipt."

"Interesting. Did it feel like she was hiding something?" Luke asked.

"We're all hiding something. I just wondered if she was buying it as a gift or heirloom or to use occasionally, like for protection and stuff. But it was an old one. I didn't think it could still work," the lady said.

Luke nodded slowly, but his brain was working fast. He narrowed down to two suspects: Mark's ex-girlfriend Faith, or his mistress, Queen. He had to meet both.

13

———————

"YOU'RE the first person I've met that's growing an entire forest inside their home," Luke said as he marvelled at the variety of plants he was looking at. His host, Mark's ex-girlfriend Faith, grinned widely. She wore an apron and rubber gloves, which were stained with dirt.

"Everyone says the seedlings are so many that they should pay the rent. That's when I tell them they've been paying the rent for the past three years," Faith replied with a grin.

Luke smiled. "This is impressive. How does your son feel about it?"

"Well, he's outside playing with his friends instead of helping, so that tells you everything," Faith said.

They laughed.

"I guess when this is all over, I'll make an order for some seedlings. I'm moving into a new place," Luke said.

"That's nice. What kind of place? Space is important for plants. That's why instead of living in an apartment, I chose this two-bedroom bungalow," she said.

"I'm keeping it pretty basic. A one-bedroomed place will

work for me, and an apartment is cheaper. I'm starting over after my divorce," he said.

"Oh. Sorry to hear that," she said. "Welcome to the single life."

Luke nodded. He had visited as a potential client, but now had to drop his cover.

"Thanks. Now that we're there, I have to admit I'm not just here to talk about the seedlings. I'm here to talk about Mark," Luke said.

Her gaze darkened. "Who are you?"

"I'm a private investigator. I'm here to find out who killed Mark. Do you mind if I asked you a few questions?" he asked.

She shook her head. "I think you should leave."

"Hear me out. I'm trying to help you. You come across as calm and collected, and you need to think rationally. Someone shot up your ex. Trust me, the police might look into you," Luke said.

"Why would they look into me? We broke up a while back," Faith said.

"So you're telling me you felt nothing when he died?" Luke asked.

"I felt for my son, who loved his father. I don't know how he'll handle it when I finally tell him. Other than that, we had a complicated arrangement that I won't miss," Faith said.

"Your relationship with him wasn't smooth, was it?" Luke asked.

"Well, I have a child with him, so that's never smooth. But I stayed away from him and Lynda. They kept coming after me," she said.

"In what ways?"

"He was accusing me of poisoning his son's mind. That

was messed up. But even more messed up is his wife threatening me," she said.

"Threatening you with what?" he asked.

"To hurt me if I didn't leave him alone. But how do I do that when the son needs a father? She needed to grow up, but now it's a little too late. He's gone," Faith said.

"So, will you make peace with her?" Luke asked.

"Make peace for what? Let's just respect each other from a distance," Faith replied.

"I read somewhere that you once defaced his car with a key," Luke said.

Faith sighed. "When we were together, we had a toxic relationship. We hurt each other in ways I'm not keen to talk about. But I've worked on my anger issues. Nothing would ever drive me up the wall. I'd never take my son's father away from him like that. He didn't deserve that."

"Where were you the day he died?" Luke asked.

"I was at the salon the whole day. You can check with them," Faith said. She handed him a business card. Mabella Beauty Care. "Anything else?"

"Not at the moment. I'll be coming for the seedlings," Luke said.

"I'll only deal with you next time when it's business related. Right now, I've got a lot to focus on," Faith said.

"I hear you. Thanks for your time."

Luke felt tired as he drove back to the motel. He took a cold shower. He then sat on the motel bed in his bathrobe watching the television, but lost in his thoughts.

He had an hour till his next engagement: a date with a woman in her late twenties that he met through the dating app. There was an urge to cancel, but he also found the atmosphere in the motel suffocating. He needed a fresh stimulus, and she might offer that.

He dressed smart casual, with a black khaki shirt and pants, brown shoes, and a corduroy jacket. Nothing to make him feel too serious. He wanted to manage his expectations this time.

He arrived at the Oephia rooftop restaurant overlooking WestBay City, which offered a great scenic view of the cityscape as the sun went down. He got there five minutes before their meeting time, and she showed up three minutes later. She was elegant in an evening dress and a little half coat. Her smile was radiant, and he was taken by her even before she said hello.

"Lelo, right?" Luke asked as he rose to receive her.

"Yeah. Luke?"

"You got me. Nice to meet you," he replied.

"I was a little worried you'd be much taller," she said.

"I'm wearing my flat shoes, so you're lucky," he teased.

They sat and ordered some beef bobotie and chicken curry.

"Do you often arrive early for dates?" she asked as she dug into her beef bobotie, a baked casserole made from minced beef, various curries, and an egg custard on top. Luke's South Indian chicken curry was made just the way he liked it, with whole spices and generous gravy.

"This is actually my second date in a long time. I think arriving early is a good thing to ease me into it," Luke said.

"Ah, I see. Social anxiety?" she asked.

"That's not something I fully understand, but I'm getting the hang of this dating thing again. I recently separated from my wife," Luke said.

"Wife or ex-wife?" Lelo asked.

"Ex-wife. We just completed our divorce process," Luke said.

"Ah, I see. How long were you married?"

"Seven years," Luke said.

"Wow. What broke you up?" Lelo said.

Luke sighed as he scooped some more curry. "We drifted apart."

"Really? No cheating or anything sinister?" she asked.

Luke glanced at her for a moment, then shook his head. "No, we were both secure in our relationship. At least to the best of my knowledge. We just realised we were both growing in different directions."

"Are you sure you've healed from it?" Lelo asked.

Luke put down his fork and wiped his mouth with his napkin. He leaned back in his seat.

"Why so many questions?" he asked.

"Does it bother you?" Lelo said.

"Yes, it does now, so just stop. What do you do when not going on dates?" Luke asked.

She wiped her lips with her napkin. He noticed she left a light trace of red lipstick on it.

"I'm a therapist by profession," she replied.

"What do you mean, a therapist?" he asked.

"I listen to people's worries and help them push through their life struggles," she replied. "This includes couples."

Luke narrowed his eyes. "How long have you practised?"

"Several years," Lelo replied.

"I see. Is it possible to leave work at home for this date?" he prodded.

She sighed. "Unfortunately not. And I must admit, this is one issue I'm facing while I date. Maybe it's something I need to work on. But I need to know the person I'm meeting and try to get an idea of what space they are in before I commit."

"You do this with all your dates or just some?" he asked.

"I do it with people I really like," she said.

"Okay, I'm no therapist but I'll tell you this: it's ruining the night," Luke said.

"I know, and I apologise. Frankly, I feel you're not ready to date either," she said.

"Excuse me?"

"You should give yourself some time to heal before you get back on the market. Something about you feels fragile to me," Lelo replied.

"You don't trust my intentions?" he asked.

"Even if I took it in good faith, I can't trust you because I barely know you," she said.

They both went silent for about a minute as they stared outside, their meals temporarily forgotten. The city's night-lights were a beautiful sight, and gave a brief respite to what they'd just said to each other.

"Thank you for the meal, but I think I have to leave," Lelo said.

She rose. As she turned to leave, she said, "If anything changes in a few months, let me know. I might be open to another date. I'll be working on my stuff too, so I'll be able to make it up to you with a better date and conversation."

"All right. Thanks for coming out," he said. "Do you want to pack the food?"

"No, that's fine. I'll make it up to you. Enjoy your evening," Lelo said, and walked off.

Luke glanced at his watch. The date had lasted just twenty-five minutes. It impressed him that the restaurant served them so fast, but it also rivalled his first date in terms of brevity.

He finished his meal in silence, punctuated by the chatter of other guests and the soft jazz playing from the overhead speakers. The view outside calmed him down and he later ordered an apple cider, which he sipped as he enjoyed the sights.

His phone rang. It was Cindi.

"Hey, am I interrupting your lovely night?" she asked.

"Only a good view. What's up?"

"I just got a tip about George's recent activities. You won't believe this, but a month ago he signed up for shooting classes at a local gun range. He's been trying out hand guns more recently," she said.

Luke sat up straight. "Are you serious?"

"Very serious."

"Why does George, a loner, need a gun?" Luke asked out loud. "Unless he's learning how to kill."

14

———————

LUKE HAD BEEN TRYING to reach Queen, Mark's alleged mistress, for two days. She'd been difficult to find. When she picked his call, she was evasive. He had to use all his charm to convince her to meet him. She shared her address.

The Velum Apartments were less fancy than Luke expected. Tucked away amongst the more luxury high rises in Northville, its seven floors stood out for its faded cream wall paint.

He confirmed his suspicions when he found the lift wasn't working. He had to make the slow climb to the fourth floor. The corridors were at least illuminated despite having little natural sunlight coming in. He knocked on the door of Apartment B14.

A peep hole opened in the middle of the door and a young woman's voice filtered through.

"Who is it?" she asked.

"Luke. We spoke on the phone."

A woman in her early twenties opened. Her hair was tied back in a ponytail. She wore a fitting top and jeans, accentuating her curvy figure. She gave him the once over as if to confirm he wasn't a threat, then stepped aside.

"Come in," Queen said.

Her apartment was small but decent. Sparsely furnished, she had a settee and bean bags for furniture. A large flat TV hung on the wall, flanked by hefty speakers. The opposite wall had a colourful abstract painting. A round carpet covered the centre of the floor.

"Make yourself comfortable," she said. "You want anything?"

"Tea?" he asked.

"I don't drink tea. So maybe apple juice or water?" she offered.

"Water sounds good," Luke replied.

Queen got a drinking glass from the cabinet, walked over to the water dispenser, and filled it up. She handed it to him.

"So, you're a private investigator, you said?" Queen asked.

"Yes, and I'm here to help you," Luke replied. "Have you spoken to the police yet?"

"Not yet. Am I supposed to?" Queen asked. "I don't need that right now."

"Well, that's why I'm here. So that you don't have to," Luke said.

"Okay. What would you like to know?" Queen asked.

"We only touched on this on the phone, but it's clear that you knew Mark," Luke said.

Queen nodded without a word.

"Do you want to tell me about that?" Luke asked, avoiding a leading question that would make her more defensive.

"We met at a friend's house party. My friend was leaving

the country and asked us to celebrate with them. During the party, Mark walked up to me as I hung out with a few friends. We exchanged numbers and everything else started from there," Queen said.

"What do you mean by everything?" Luke asked.

Queen sighed. "We got to know each other better. He liked me, I liked him. We got close."

"Did you know he was married?" Luke asked.

Queen shook her head. "No. He never wore a wedding ring and never talked about his wife. We were just connecting and enjoying ourselves. It was a difficult time for me when we met, as I'd just started looking for a job after college. So he helped me out a lot."

He could hear her voice getting shaky, but he wasn't sure if it was out of fear or loss.

"He meant a lot to you?"

Queen smiled, then went quiet. A tear rolled down her cheek, and she wiped it off.

"Excuse me," she said as she got up and left. She returned a minute later with a handkerchief.

"Yes, he meant a lot to me. We cared about each other. There's no need to hide that. Maybe if I knew he was married from the beginning, I'd have backed out. But I loved him, and I can't deny that. This whole thing is messed up," Queen said.

"I'm sorry for your loss. Where are you working now?" he asked.

"I got a job at a casino. He helped me with that," she said.

"Good to hear. When did you find out he was married?" he asked.

"About a month ago. He let it slip when we were right

here watching a movie. We argued a bit and then he left. Things weren't the same after that," she said.

"What do you mean?" Luke asked.

"We weren't talking the way we used to. I don't come from a family that had a lot, so getting my life on track is my chance to make a difference. I can't afford to sleep with a married man," she replied.

"Did it make you angry that he deceived you?" Luke said.

"Of course it did. It showed he didn't respect me," she said. "When he'd give me money, I thought he was appreciating me. After that, it was like he was trying to buy my trust. I didn't need that."

Luke could tell she wanted to straighten out her life, and Mark was a benefactor. However, there were lines she didn't want to cross, even if Mark wanted to. She wouldn't lose herself to him.

"You sound like you have goals for yourself and keeping your life simple is a good way to go," Luke said. "You don't need the drama that an affair brings your way."

Queen nodded.

"I just want to do things differently, for the sake of my family," she said. "No one in my family knows about this and I'd like it to stay that way."

"I'll do my part. If it's okay, I'll be checking in on you once in a while," Luke said.

Queen didn't respond, twiddling her thumbs instead.

He left, feeling a little guilty for even meeting her. She deserved better.

As he walked down the stairs after leaving her apartment, Luke concluded Queen couldn't afford nor think of buying a rare gun. He had to look elsewhere for the killer.

His mother's house was close to the Velum Apartments, so he passed by to greet her.

His relationship with his mother intrigued him. Mable was a principled, energetic woman. While she'd been strict with him while growing up, their relationship had mellowed to a level where he'd freely tease and have tough conversations with her. She often wore a headscarf, t-shirt and pleated skirt, an old school look that she couldn't shake off. He visited every week to get updates on family projects and to taste her food. Recent conversations had been revolving around children, and today wasn't an exception.

"When are you giving me grandkids?" she asked.

"Soon, Ma. Be patient. I have to prepare for them, you know," he said.

"You'll never be ready. Do you think I was ready when I gave birth to you? I wasn't. Yet here you are, thriving," Mable commented.

"There's no hurry. I've still got time," he said.

"Time for what? You're in your forties. Can't you see the older you get, the more likely you'll be taking a teen to school when you're in your fifties?" Mable said.

"It will be fine. Stop the fear mongering," Luke replied.

"How's Helen doing?" Mable asked.

"She's doing well, Ma. But we're both moving on with our lives and I don't see that changing soon," Luke said.

"Well, you could marry Gladys Mokoena. She's about your age and is a fantastic teacher. Or Alice Thuti, she's running a great business downtown. They're both looking for someone," she said.

"Get me their numbers and then I'll take it from there," Luke said as he stood to leave. "I've got to run. I have a date."

Mable beamed. "You're letting me waste all this oxygen, yet you have a date? Who is she?"

"It's going to be our first date, so I've got no idea who she is. Wish me luck," Luke said.

"Have another cup of tea as we talk about this," she said as she headed to the kitchen.

"Honestly, I can't stay. You want me to date someone, right? Then I have to keep time," he said.

"All right, my son. But you'll tell me how it goes?"

"If she behaves, of course. Thanks for the bites, Ma," he said as he walked out the front door of her house into the afternoon sunlight.

After freshening up at the motel, Luke arrived at the Chip Palace wearing the most casual outfit he could find; jeans, a baseball jacket, and sneakers.

The fast-food restaurant was half-full, with several empty tables where he could wait for his date, Mpumi. He knew she was in her early thirties, which was right about his target age. Her text messages had a maturity about them that intrigued him. She sounded excited when he called her, so he expected some energy.

Sure enough, when she arrived, he heard her shout a jovial "Luke!" from across the room.

She cantered to where he sat, and before he could stand up, hugged him tight.

"It's so good to see you!" Mpumi said as she pulled back.

"Same here," Luke replied. She pulled back, and he got a good look at her. She was cute, with bright wide eyes and a rich smile.

She sat across from him and looked at the blank table. "You haven't ordered yet?"

"No, I was waiting for you," Luke replied.

"Oh, okay. Then let's go somewhere else," she said.

"Excuse me?" Luke asked.

"Let's go somewhere else. There's a nice amusement

park close to here. We can have some fun there," Mpumi said.

Luke feigned a smile. "What kind of fun are you talking about?"

"There are so many things we can do. There's food there, and then we can walk around and see what's interesting. I know we'll find something that works for you. Wanna go?" she asked.

Luke felt increasingly old at this point. These were the things he'd hoped to do with his family, not a date. He was tempted to go back to the motel, but he also knew he wouldn't get very far in the dating scene without trying new things. It might be fun. What could go wrong?

"Sure, let's do it," he said.

"Yes!" Mpumi said as she pumped her fist in the air.

They left in Luke's car, a fifteen-minute drive to the theme park. Luke parked in the car park, and they walked through the park's enormous gates on foot.

It was a weekday afternoon, and Luke thought there would be a few people at the place. However, there was a decent crowd of people walking around the place and using the attractions. There were lush gardens, restaurants, snack bars, giant tents for circus acts, park rides, and two Ferris wheels.

They went to the restaurant first, where they ate some Mexican tacos and fresh juices before heading for the rides, which Mpumi kept talking about.

"That Ferris wheel is the best. I wish they'd build a roller coaster ride, but for now the Ferris wheel will do," she said.

"Why do you want to go so high?" Luke asked.

"So that I can see the world differently," she said. "I forget everything. Even my worries become smaller when I'm up there."

Luke hated heights, but he wanted his problems to feel smaller. He signed up for the Ferris wheel ride. They had to wait for half an hour, which they spent shooting water balloons. Mpumi won a small teddy bear. She gave it to a random child, which amused Luke.

Their turn came, and they got onto the Ferris wheel. To his relief, he was told that it wouldn't move fast.

As the wheel started moving, Luke tried his best to forget his fear of heights and focus on the beauty of the scenery. Mpumi offered excited commentary about what she was seeing.

"You see how big this city is? I think we should build a better train system. Imagine we had fast trains here..."

As she rambled on and on, Luke got lost in his thoughts. He wondered how long it would take to solve the case. Would he have enough money to finish it?

They soon got to the highest point of the wheel's movement, and he didn't want to look down. He gripped the safety bar tightly as he braced for the descent.

He felt a nudge.

"Luke, help me put this back on," Mpumi said as she held up her seat belt. It had loosened from its buckle.

He leaned over but couldn't reach her without unbuckling himself. He quickly did this and leaned over. After a little troubleshooting, he buckled her seat belt.

When he settled back into his position, the angle of the double-seat changed, and he leaned forward. Instead of holding him, the safety bar gave way. Before he could comprehend what was happening, Luke felt weightless as he flew off the seat and into the air.

He was falling.

15

IN A SPLIT MOMENT, Luke's mind rushed back to his childhood, to the one dream he hated the most. The dream where he was falling down a dark flight of stairs. His hands would flail wildly, and he'd be screaming, and there'd be no one to help. He'd fall endlessly without reaching the bottom–until he woke up.

Wake up.

He heard the voice. It was sharp.

Grab it.

He turned to see his body moving past the footrest of the double-seat.

Grab it!

His left hand quickly grabbed the footrest. He could suddenly hear Mpumi screaming.

"Oh my God, oh my God," she said with one hand over her mouth as tears rolled down her face.

Luke could also hear the other riders gasping and shouting, but all their voices were in the background of what he wanted to hear. The only voice he was obeying was the inner voice. The others be damned.

His left hand supported his weight as he swung from side to side like a pendulum.

Grab it.

He knew what that meant. His left hand was the weaker one, and his best chance of survival was to hold the footrest with both hands. He timed the swing that brought up his right side towards the double seat and made a lunge. He barely made it, grabbing the metal with three fingers before adding the rest. But he now had a better grip.

They slowly lowered the Ferris wheel, and Luke did his best to hang on. It stopped several feet from the ground, and he had to wait for two more minutes as they placed a large inflated mattress under him so that he could jump to the ground.

"Let go," he heard someone below him shout.

He didn't need a second prompt. He released his hold and landed on the large mattress.

Security guards and paramedics immediately surrounded him and they lay him on the ground to assess his condition.

"I'm fine, honestly," Luke kept saying, although he felt an intense pain in both his wrists.

It took half an hour before they released him. They had massaged both wrists with soothing ointment and advised him to do the same when he got home, otherwise he'd wake up to find them swollen.

He saw Mpumi seated on a bench. As he walked towards her, the small crowd that had formed cheered and clapped for him. He waved in appreciation, although he felt responsible for the error.

He eased himself next to Mpumi, who was licking one of the largest lollipops he had ever seen.

"They say I'm great. Thanks for asking," Luke said.

"I was right here through it all, rooting for you," Mpumi said.

"A little difficult to feel it from that distance," Luke remarked.

"I don't handle trauma very well," Mpumi said.

Luke frowned. "Trauma? My wrists hurt a little, that's all."

"I'm talking about that moment you had to hang on to that thing. It tore me to pieces," she replied.

"I see. Is that why you're having the largest lollipop I've ever seen?" he asked.

"This is how I cope with stress. They didn't have the ice cream flavour I wanted, so I settled for this," Mpumi replied.

They sat in silence for a few more minutes.

"Can we go somewhere else?" Luke asked.

Mpumi turned to him.

"I've been thinking that this was a terrible start. This already feels jinxed. I can't shake off what just happened. So I need to heal, and I think you need to heal, too. You know, to get over the event," Mpumi said.

Luke chuckled. "Heal from what? I'm fine!"

"No, you're not. And even if you are, I'm not. I've got some crazy fears that got triggered by this event. I need time," she said.

Luke looked into her eyes. They were teary, and she blinked fast. Her happy-go-lucky nature had disappeared, and all he saw was pure fear.

"Alright, I hear you. Can I drop you off somewhere?" he asked.

"No, I'll take a taxi," Mpumi said as she rose to her feet. "It was nice meeting you. Take care of yourself."

As he watched her retreat into the distance, he laughed. He did this for a few minutes. It wasn't something he was doing out of joy, but mild amusement at the joke he called a dating life. He had no tools and no luck so far, and he found the level of failure he had experienced amusing.

"Maybe this dating thing isn't for me," he muttered under his breath.

Luke sat there for a short while and decided that maybe Mpumi was right. He needed help, and that meant talking to someone. He resolved to see a psychiatrist.

Early the next morning, at fifteen minutes past eight, Luke sat in Doctor Walter Wendosi's reception. Maybe George's own psychiatrist could offer some professional insights while giving Luke some clues that would help him understand what was going on in George's mind.

He'd already booked a one-hour session; he was simply waiting for the doctor to arrive.

Walter arrived at exactly 8.30 a.m., wearing a half sweater, long-sleeved shirt and well-pressed cotton trousers with shiny black shoes. He gave a jovial greeting to the receptionist, who pointed Luke out. The smiling doctor walked up to him and held out his hand.

"Hello there. You're here to see me?" Walter asked.

"Yes, sir. A friend had recommended you to me," Luke replied.

"Excellent. I rarely take walk-in clients, but today is your lucky day. I have a light schedule this morning. Follow me," Walter said.

Walter's office was a haven. It was furnished to be cosy and help you forget the outside world exists. There was a thick carpet across the floor that made Luke feel like he was walking on air. Although there was a desk, it was medium-sized, polished and decked with images of his family – a wife and two little children. The windows had large curtains which were partially drawn so that the corner lights could illuminate the room with a relaxing hue.

"Please, take a seat on that couch," Walter said as he pointed to a lush leather couch. As he eased himself into it, Luke felt like he was out of place. The therapist he and his ex-wife had seen before they divorced had an austere office. Maybe if they'd done their marriage counselling sessions with Walter, it might have saved their union using the ambience alone, he mused.

"Are you sure this is where we're going to do the session?" Luke asked.

"Of course. You don't like it?" Walter asked.

"I always thought you guys had more bland offices," Luke said.

"Well, I do things differently. The healing starts here, where you can relax and let out what's troubling you," Walter said in a soothing, eloquent voice. "Tell me about yourself."

Luke introduced himself but avoided giving any personal information about his past. Instead, he focused on his recent troubles with dating.

"The general feedback I'm getting is that I have stuff to sort out within myself. Frankly, I feel fine. Sure, I'm more cautious about things after my last relationship, but I don't think it's a deal breaker," Luke said.

Walter scribbled in his notebook, and then leaned back in his chair, resting his chin on his right palm.

"What I'm getting from what you're saying is that you still have some unresolved issues from a previous relationship. Did you break up recently?" Walter asked.

"Divorced, actually. I still have visitation rights for our dog," Luke said.

Walter's eyes narrowed. "But the dog isn't the family you wanted, is it?"

Luke sighed, surprised by Walter's insight. "No, it isn't. It was just supposed to be a part of the puzzle. We both wanted a child. We were to live on a farm somewhere and raise our kids."

"Who had the problem? You or her?"

Luke scowled. "Does it matter?"

"It does. It means one of you is carrying the guilt of failing the relationship," Walter replied.

"We both did. She had a miscarriage that had her in the hospital for a few weeks. She was never the same after that. I didn't know how to handle it, and we slowly drifted apart. We became strangers under the same roof. It was better to start over," Luke said.

Walter scribbled some more. "And you're afraid of committing again, right?"

"Afraid is a strong word. I'm cautious and rusty. It's been a while since I went on a date," Luke said.

"Uncertainty is not a good thing to start new relationships with. You've got to clear that baggage before you're free to let someone else in." Walter replied.

Luke nodded. "You know what? You're right. It's not a good look. It makes me paranoid sometimes, and it's hard to connect with the real world."

"Yes, it is. Luckily, I've had a few patients dealing with something similar and I helped them get better. You'll be fine, too," Walter said with a smile.

"Patients like George West?" Luke asked.

Walter frowned. "How do you know George West?"

"He's the friend who recommended you to me," Luke replied. "He's one of your patients, right?"

"Yes, he is, and I'm glad that he wants you to get better," Walter replied.

"Is he making progress himself?"

Walter tilted his head. "Why do you ask?"

"Well, I guess I just want to know someone familiar is getting the help they need," Luke said.

"You interact with him... Have you seen any improvements in his life recently?" Walter inquired.

Luke pretended to be reflecting on this question. "A bit. But he's still, what shall I say, living in suspended reality."

Walter raised a brow. "What do you mean?"

"I mean, he still fantasises about scenarios that shouldn't happen. Dangerous acts of violence. I'm sure he's told you about them, right?" Luke said. He leaned back, watching Walter's reaction.

Walter fidgeted in his seat, crossing his left leg over his right. "I'm not at liberty to talk about what other patients tell me. But there's still some work to do with him."

"You can't tell me if he's at least overcome his violent urges?" Luke asked.

"I can neither confirm nor deny he's told me such things. How do you know George again?" Walter queried.

"Our families knew each other while growing up," Luke lied. "We bump into each other once in a while. So you can't tell me more?"

Walter shook his head and closed his notebook. "No, I can't, unfortunately. I believe our time is up."

Luke frowned and glanced at his wristwatch. "We still have twenty minutes to go."

Walter feigned a smile. "This session needs to focus on you, not on other patients. So go home and reflect on some things you would like to change for yourself. We can then schedule another session and extend it by twenty minutes."

Luke sighed and rose. "Thanks. That was refreshing, frankly. Until next time."

"Until next time," Walter replied.

Luke left with the lingering feeling that Walter ended the session early because talking about George was uncomfortable. He knew that he'd call George and ask if he knew him, so the chances of getting another session were slim. Luke would have to put him on the spot using other means.

With the afternoon ahead of him, Luke drove to the shooting school that George was attending. The Uxaba Shooting Academy office was a prefabricated building that had two floors. Its exterior walls had seen better days with peeling paint as a standout feature. A clearing that was bordered by trees surrounded it. Some trees had visible bullet scrapes and holes. Strangely, others had chunks of missing bark.

Luke parked in the gravel car park next to two vandalised car shells and a rickety *bakkie* pickup with bald tyres. The car park also had shrubs here and there, an indication that either the owner preferred a rugged look or the place was run down. Luke put on his coat and combed his hair before stepping out of the car.

When he got to the reception, it was pristine, with a fan blowing overhead, a television showing the day's news, and a pleasant smiley receptionist behind a fibreglass desk.

"How may I help you, sir?" The receptionist asked warmly.

"Hello. I'm Inspector Wallace from the Kedoe Police Station. I'd like to speak to the manager," Luke said.

The receptionist's smile quickly disappeared. "Can I ask what this is about?"

"Just tell him I have a few questions to ask him," Luke replied.

As the receptionist nervously called her manager, Luke gently tapped the top of the reception desk.

Moments later, a grey-haired man in his fifties emerged from a door.

He held out his hand to Luke. "Hello officer. I'm Hillary Bragg, the manager here. How can I help you?"

"I'm Inspector Wallace from the Kedoe Police Station. Is George West a client of yours?" Luke asked.

Hillary nodded. "Yes, he is. Why?"

"I'd like to see his records first, and then I'll tell you why," Luke said.

"What records?" Hillary asked.

"Everything you've got," Luke replied.

"That material is confidential," Hillary said.

Luke walked up to Hillary and placed his right arm on his left shoulder.

"I have a feeling you don't want to be accused of obstructing a murder investigation. Do you?" Luke whispered.

He could feel Hillary tense up under his grip.

16

———

"ARE you going to help me or not?" Luke asked Hillary.

"Did George kill someone?" Hillary asked.

"That hasn't been confirmed, although your help can help answer that question," Luke said.

Hillary nodded and led him into the adjacent room. It was a small office with a desk, two seats, a notice board, a whiteboard, and a steel office cabinet.

Hillary walked to the cabinet, opened it. He took a minute to sift through them, then returned with a file.

"This is George's file. It has his progress records since he came here," Hillary said.

Luke took the file and leafed through it. It had fifteen pages. The first one had George's personal information, while the remaining pages were for the various shooting modules he was being trained on.

"How many sessions does he attend per week?" Luke asked.

"Well, he's not been able to attend recent classes due to cash issues, but on average he'd come for two one-hour classes every week," Hillary replied.

"For the past six months?" Luke asked.

"Yes, for the past six months," Hillary said. "He's been pretty consistent."

"In attendance, you mean," Luke said as he leafed through the pages. "These records don't look very consistent nor progressive in terms of marksmanship."

Hillary sighed. "Well, he had his moments. He struggled a lot with weapon handling, shooting in hard conditions and ultimately his accuracy."

"So, how is he on an ideal day?" Luke asked.

"He's just scraping by average," Hillary said.

"Meaning what?"

"I wouldn't give him any gun at the moment. Even on a good day, he's more likely to hurt himself or someone by accident," Hillary replied.

"Are we talking about hand guns or rifles?" Luke asked.

"Both. Look, I don't mean to be rude or anything, but he's pretty hopeless. I don't know why he wants to learn how to shoot. Although his mind is set on it, I just can't see it happening," Hillary said.

Luke nodded. He held up the file. "I'll need to go with this."

Hillary shook his head. "What for?"

"Evidence," Luke replied.

"But you haven't even shown me your identification," Hillary said.

Luke pursed his lips. "It's a murder investigation. The less you know, the better. Please, don't be tempted to tell anyone about this, including George. It could jeopardise the investigation."

Before Hillary could argue, Luke was already out of the door.

Luke walked back to the car. He spotted a grey squirrel

near one of his rear tyres. He slowed down and watched it. It was nibbling at a nut in its forelimbs, oblivious to his presence. Even as he took two more steps toward it, it didn't budge. It was so absorbed in its meal that he formed a theory. It had tunnel vision such that all it wanted to do was finish the snack.

Then it hit him: was he also suffering the same thing? Why was he so focused on George? Now that it was obvious someone else other than George was the shooter, was it possible that he was letting the real killer slip away?

What if George hired a killer? If he was such a poor shot, then someone else must have murdered Mark.

Faith could've pulled it off, too. If Mark was already a shooting enthusiast when they were together, had he taught her how to fire a gun? Luke didn't know this, but it was worth looking into. Still, she could have also hired an assassin to do the job for her. She also had a bone to pick with Mark and Lynda, and her anger issues may have pushed her over the edge.

Luke looked up towards the squirrel, but it had scooted away while he was lost in his thoughts. Luke got into his car and sat for a few minutes, wondering if he should talk to Faith again or give George one last nudge. He decided it was better to keep the pressure on George. He might break.

He arrived at George's house and found his dilapidated sedan parked out front. He walked to the door and gave it a hard knock.

"Open up, George. I need to have a word," Luke said.

Nothing.

He knocked again. This time, the door opened, but only by a crack.

"What do you want?" George asked.

"I've got a few more questions to ask you," Luke said.

"I said all I needed to say," George replied.

"I'm here to help you," Luke replied.

"I don't need your help, so please leave," George said as he closed the door. Luke jammed his foot in the door.

"Do you have someone else in there?" Luke asked.

"What if I do? It's none of your business," George replied.

But Luke had met no other people in George's life, so this was a good chance as any.

"Let me in. It will only be a few minutes," Luke said, craning his neck. He couldn't see anything inside.

"That will not happen," George said as he started pushing out Luke's foot.

Luke wasn't having it, and he pushed back with all his might, forcing his way in.

17

———————

THE FORCE of Luke's push had George stumbling over himself. He fell in a heap as Luke stepped in. A woman screamed.

She was in her mid-twenties, bespectacled and wore sweat pants.

"Call the police, Shea!" George said as he got to his feet.

"What's going on, Georgie?" the young woman asked.

"Calm your horses. Don't make that mistake, young lady. He's not who you think he is," Luke said as he shut the door behind him.

"What is he talking about, Georgie?" Shea asked.

George wrapped a reassuring arm around her shoulders. "He's just some guy who's been pestering me about the place I used to work. They won't stop bothering me. Go to the bedroom and wait for me there."

"Are you sure you want to stay in the same house as a stalker? He'll never give you the peace and fun you want," Luke said.

George frothed. "Shut up! You don't know what you're talking about."

"I'm not lying. Show her the room, George," Luke said.

George's eyes blazed with rage.

"What room?" Shea asked.

"Don't worry about it, it's nothing," George said.

"Show her the room behind the shelf," Luke said.

"What room? I want to know," Shea said as she got out of his hold.

George dropped his head. He didn't budge.

"George, are you showing me this room or not?" Shea asked.

"I can't," George mumbled.

Shea shook her head, dashed into the bedroom, and returned with her bag over her shoulder.

"I want nothing to do with this. Lose my number," Shea said as she marched to the door. She slammed the door behind her.

The two men stood still in the hallway as they heard her footfalls disappear down the street.

"Now it's just the two of us, the way it's supposed to be," Luke said.

"What do you want?" George asked.

"To see the room. You can hide it from her, but you can't hide it from me. Then you can explain to me why you've got all those pictures," Luke said.

George scowled at Luke. "I don't have to do anything you tell me. You're trespassing, just like last time."

"You'll want to rethink that stance if you want to avoid jail. You don't know what information I've shared with the cops. It's in your best interests to work with me instead of against me," Luke replied.

George stood his ground. Luke sighed and began rolling up his sleeves.

"What do you think you're doing?" George asked.

"Helping you," Luke replied. He strode to George, grabbed him by the collar and yanked him towards the bookshelf.

"Open it. Now!" Luke ordered.

The now meek George didn't resist and they were soon inside the small room. It was exactly the same way as Luke had first seen it, including the photos on the wall.

"Care to tell me why Mark and Lynda have bull's-eyes on their heads?" Luke asked.

"They were dead to me. Nothing more than that," George said.

"Sounds more like you wanted them dead. Who did you hire to kill Mark?" Luke asked.

"I didn't hire anybody. I don't have the money for that kind of thing," George said.

"Hatred doesn't care about resources. All it wants is to achieve its aim. And you achieved the first one, didn't you?" Luke prodded.

"I didn't do it," George said.

"You realise if I bring the cops in here, you're going behind bars for life? You'd better tell me what happened now. I might put in a good word for you," Luke said.

Luke felt George's shoulders shaking and then he realised the man was sobbing.

"I didn't do it," George said, followed by sniffling. Luke loosened his grip on the man and watched him slink into a seat. "What do I have to say to convince you?"

"Why were you taking shooting lessons?" Luke asked.

"I wanted to learn how to defend myself. Look at me. Do I look like a powerful man?" George asked.

"And where were you going to get the money to buy a gun?" Luke asked.

George shrugged. "I don't know. I didn't get that far yet. I haven't even finished my classes. My life is a mess."

George got into a fit of uncontrollable sobbing.

Luke's shoulders dropped. He hadn't intended to crush the man's spirit, but that's what he was witnessing. It was depressing, and he didn't know what to do.

"Promise me this one thing and I'll get out of your hair: you'll never talk to Lynda again. Is that clear?" Luke said.

George nodded. "I'll not follow her or call her again."

"Good. The moment you do that, I'm onto you. And if I find out you've lied to me, I'll be back," Luke said. He gave one last look at the dejected man and stepped out of the room.

Luke walked out of the house and stood for a moment. He inhaled deeply before walking slowly to his car.

With his conviction about George waning, Luke shifted his focus to Faith. She was next in line, and he wanted to do it before sunset. Although she warned him to only get in touch when it was about business, that didn't faze him. Someone was dead, and he wanted answers.

He arrived at her home at dusk, and nightlights had come on.

After ringing her bell once, the door opened.

"I'll buy one of the house plants if you answer a few of my questions," Luke said.

Faith sighed, stepped outside, and closed the door behind her. Luke figured she didn't want her son to hear their conversation. She leaned on the doorframe with her hands crossed.

"What do you want to know?" Faith asked.

"Someone laid a trap for Mark. They bought a rare gun that was used to kill him. The person who bought this knows him well, and how much he loves guns. I'm sure you know about this, right?" Luke asked.

"I know he loved guns, but I've got no idea what his favourite one is," Faith replied.

Luke raised a brow. "You were once partners. How would you not know?"

"You can know someone without liking some things about them. That's how these things work, right?" Faith said.

"So you're telling me you never went shooting with him?"

"I did, but only once and never again. I already hated the things, but you do some things for your partner. It was one of those activity dates. I made some sandwiches and fresh juice and we went to a shooting range for a couple of hours. But it just confirmed my hatred for them," Faith said.

Although what she was saying seemed plausible, Luke didn't want to write her off. If she were spiteful, she'd have still used the familiar things as bait to get him right where she wanted him. Somewhere he could die and no one would find him immediately. The more he thought about it, the more macabre it became.

"Where were you on the fourteenth of May?" Luke asked.

Faith rubbed her temple. "I can't remember, really."

"It was just a couple of weeks ago. A Saturday in the middle of May," Luke said.

Faith kept massaging her head. "It must be that Saturday I went on a drive."

"You went on a drive to where?" Luke asked.

"To nowhere really. I was just driving around to clear my head," Faith said.

"Was your son there?" Luke posed.

Faith shook her head. "No, it was a solo drive. He was at his father's place."

"Does anyone else know that you went on a drive?" Luke asked.

"Only my mother needs to know. I just got out of bed, freshened up and left," Faith said.

"I'd like to talk to her," Luke said.

"That's not gonna happen. I don't need her anywhere near this mess," Faith said.

"It can help clear your name," Luke said.

"My name is already clear, no? I had nothing to do with it?" Faith said.

Luke realised this was going nowhere.

"Very well. In case you remember something, feel free to call," Luke said.

Luke left, and as he was about to drive off, he changed his mind. Maybe their conversation had unsettled her. If she was involved, then it was only a matter of time before she left to meet her assassin. Luke monitored her movements.

An hour later, Luke had dozed off. He woke up again some minutes to midnight. After glancing at his wristwatch, he cursed under his breath. He looked outside and saw that her apartment still had a light on. He checked the notifications on his phone and found three missed calls from his mother.

He toyed with the idea of calling her at such a late hour. Then he spotted a dark form moving towards Faith's house. Luke craned his eyes to sift through the darkness. The intruder wore a black outfit and mask.

Someone was about to break into her house.

18

LUKE CAREFULLY GOT out of his car and kept to the shadows along the sidewalk until he got level with Faith's house. By this time, the intruder had started picking the lock to her front door.

Luke tiptoed towards him and then climbed the two steps to the porch. He grabbed him from behind and pulled him backwards. He somehow got down the two porch steps without falling. The man put up a fight, kicking in the air as Luke's grip tightened around his neck.

Luke spun him around and landed him on his stomach on the grassy front lawn.

"What are you doing here?" Luke whispered. He didn't want to alert Faith about the danger outside her door. The man coughed out an indiscernible response, so Luke loosened his hold slightly.

"I'll ask again: What are you doing here? Who sent you?" Luke asked.

"That's none of your business," the intruder whispered back.

Luke dug a knee into the man's back. He heard the man's low groan of pain.

"We can do this until the sun comes up. Are you sure you want that?" Luke asked. "Do you have anything to do with Mark's murder?"

"Was Mark your friend?" the man asked.

"He is now," Luke replied.

"Well, you don't know who he is. That's one reason I'd kill you. You have no clue what you're doing. Let me go and I promise they'll take it easy on you," the intruder replied.

"Who are *they* and what did they send you here for?" Luke queried.

"I'm here for a package. Mark owes us a package. Where is it?" the intruder asked.

Luke frowned. "What kind of package are we talking about?"

"What's in the package is none of your business. All we need is the package, which he didn't deliver to my boss," the intruder said.

"Does your boss know you're breaking into houses to look for the package?" Luke asked.

"He knows the nature of the business. That's why he still has me running these assignments," the man replied.

"Tell me what's in the package. It will help me find it for you," Luke said.

"I don't answer to you," the intruder replied.

"Don't make this harder than it needs to be," Luke said, tightening his grip around the intruder's neck. The man winced, but didn't answer.

"I'll ask you one more time. What package did you come for?" Luke asked.

"I don't know what was inside," the man replied.

"You're lying," Luke replied, increasing the pressure on the hold. The man groaned in agony.

Suddenly, the porch light came on. Luke spun his head just in time to see Faith pop her head from behind the door.

"Get back inside!" Luke shouted.

"Luke?" Faith said.

"I said get back inside," Luke repeated. He felt the man squirm underneath him as he tried to free himself.

Faith stepped out some more. "What's going on?"

"I'll tell you once you get back inside. I'm finishing up with this guy," Luke said.

"What did he do?" Faith asked.

"Nothing," the man muttered.

"Shut your mouth," Luke said.

"Luke, you need to let me go. If you do that, nothing will happen to you," the man replied.

Luke tightened his death grip, angered that the intruder now knew his name.

"Is that a threat?" Luke asked.

"It's a word of advice. Let me go, and I'll tell them I couldn't find it," the man said.

Luke pondered this, loosened his grip, and rose. "Get out of here."

The man got up gingerly, dusted the front of his clothes, and limped away. The dark shadows along the sidewalk soon swallowed him.

Luke turned to Faith, who stood still on her porch. "He tried to break into your house."

"How do you know that?" Faith asked.

"I saw him," Luke replied.

"You were watching my house?" Faith asked.

Luke frowned. "Yes, I was watching your house. I expected something to happen, and I was right."

Faith sighed and crossed her arms.

"He says there was a package that Mark didn't deliver. That's what he came for. Do you want to show me where that package is?" Luke asked.

Faith shrugged. "I don't know about any packages."

Luke stepped forward. "Listen, Faith. These shady people, whoever they are, know where you live. This isn't the time to play hide-and-seek. They'll hurt you if they need to. So show me where Mark used to keep his packages when they came home."

Faith buried her face in her hands. "Honest to God, I've got no idea where he'd stash them. I mean, occasionally he'd have one or two, but he never hid them. I've not seen any in recent weeks."

Luke stepped up to the porch.

"I'll need you to let me search the house," Luke said.

"For what?" Faith asked.

"For any secret compartment where Mark may have been hiding his most sensitive packages," Luke said. "Maybe the intruder was lying, and he wanted to get to you. But the only way to be sure is by ensuring Mark isn't hiding anything in the house. Otherwise, if he made the wrong people angry, they will be back, and it won't end well."

19

Klak-Klak-Klak

The rattling sound of a loose security door down the street provided an unnerving soundtrack for Luke and Faith as they stood outside her door.

"Will you let me in, or are we going to stand here all night?" Luke asked.

Faith sighed. "Alright. Come in."

She let him in and secured the door with every lock available.

"Where do you want to start?" she asked.

"You tell me," he replied.

"It's not a big house. So you can do every other room except my bedroom and my son's room. He's fast asleep," she said. "Also, try not to make a racket."

With that, she turned and went to the kitchen.

Luke started with the living room, checking under the seats and in between the cushions for false bottoms, hidden compartments, and pockets. He found none. He then moved to the walls, feeling every inch. His hands would caress the wall and then knock at the places that felt hollow. He would've done the same with the floor, but it was all concrete from wall-to-wall with no hint of disturbance.

The bookshelf, unlike George's, was also intact. This pattern continued with the bathroom and toilets. He thereafter went to the kitchen, where he found Faith whipping up a meal of rice with lamb stew.

"You didn't have to," he remarked.

"My mother taught me you need to prepare food for a visitor so long as he or she's under your roof," Faith said.

"Don't you feel odd cooking at this hour?" he asked.

"My son and I had takeaway for dinner, so the only other option was to cook. Anyway, it's nearly done. How's the search going?" she asked.

"Nothing so far. Let me check in here," Luke replied.

After fifteen minutes of carefully examining every inch of the kitchen, he came up empty.

"I have to ask you this: when did Mark come here with a secret package?" Luke said.

"That only happened once. A long time ago, I can't even remember the date," she said.

"Did you know what he was carrying?" Luke prodded.

"It was a square box wrapped in brown wrapping paper. When I asked him what was inside, he said it was better if I knew nothing about it. He was adamant about that. He never allowed me to ask him again," Faith said.

"Did you find that odd?" Luke asked.

"For a while. But since he never did it again, I stopped asking. Until recently. I think he sometimes had sensitive or illegal stuff in them that he never wanted us to know about. He didn't want to expose his son to such stuff," Faith said.

"That's it?"

"That's it. Although there was this one time where he hinted his car had a secret compartment. But he said it as a joke, and I never saw it in practise so I can't be sure," Faith said.

She lifted the lid off the lamb stew, and a salivating-inducing aroma filled the room.

"It's time to eat," she announced in a lively hushed tone.

The meal was so tasty it had Luke licking his lips and belching with satisfaction. They talked about the case, parenthood and any random thing that came to their minds. Luke felt like he was catching up with an old friend, something he hadn't expected.

"Tell me something: what kept you hanging around long after you left my house?" Faith asked.

"A hunch. Something told me I needed to stay put and watch your back. It seems I was right," Luke replied.

Faith smiled. "It's been a while since I felt a man was looking out for me. It can be lonely, especially for a single mum."

"Mark didn't come over often?" he asked.

"He did, mostly on weekends. But it was for his son, which is great. He's our lifeblood. But sometimes I want someone to look out for me, too," Faith said.

"I hear you. Although I don't have kids. It used to be the dog I would visit. But after a while, you feel hollow. Then I realised I need someone else to pour into me so that I can keep showing other people love," Luke said.

"Do you have someone?"

"I'm recently divorced. Just tried getting back into the dating scene. It's been a disaster so far," Luke said.

"*Eish.* Love sucks," Faith said.

"No, love is good. Dating is what sucks," Luke said.

They both laughed.

"I don't think we have to look at it through such a dark lens," Luke replied.

"So much labour for what?" Faith asked.

Luke grunted. "I look at it this way: you grew because of connecting with that person. Assuming it wasn't totally toxic, of course. If you grew, then you become better for the next person."

"But the clock is ticking. Life isn't a rehearsal. I can't keep trying out guys as if it's the lottery and hoping for the best," she said.

"You need to know who you are first. Do you know who you are, Faith?" he asked.

"Now you're making this about me?" she said.

"It's always been about you. It's not about who is messing you up. Something in you is attracting the wrong guy and you need to address that first," Luke said.

Faith fidgeted. "You talk so boldly about me, yet you barely know me."

Luke raised his hands in mock surrender. "Sorry, I thought we were analysing both our approaches. That same thing applies to me. I can't seem to find someone, and I guess it's because I've changed and I've not got acquainted with this new version of me."

Without warning, Faith's left hand reached for Luke's hand and stroked it gently. "Did your old self always take risks like your new self does?"

Luke could feel the odd sensation that her light touch delivered to his body, but he didn't flinch.

"He did, just differently. What are you doing?" Luke asked.

Faith pulled back her hand quickly and then rose to her feet.

"I'm sorry about that. Silly of me. I'll go up and get a sweater," Faith said.

Before he could interject, she was already heading for the stairs.

Luke smiled. She'd clearly made a pass at him, something he didn't expect. Strangely enough, he also didn't mind it. In his opinion, it was a good sign that she was trusting him. The closer he could get, the more likely he'd learn more and possibly crack the case.

His eyes landed on her laptop, which was on a computer desk in a corner of the room. It was open, with the screensaver of the Cape Flats. He glanced up the stairs before walking to the computer desk. He leaned over and touched the mouse. The screen came alive as it wasn't password protected. Besides a news article and a paused cooking video on how to make flat bread, no other windows were open.

He searched her browser history, curious to see if there was anything interesting. It had been set to clear every twenty-four hours, so there was nothing to see other than links to several cooking websites.

His eyes wandered to the Documents section, and he started browsing the folders.

"What are you doing?" Faith asked.

Like a child caught with his hands in the cookie jar, Luke turned fast to look at her. She stood in front of him, dressed in a warm sweater that fell loosely over her shoulders, with a sullen face.

"I was just checking to see if I could email," Luke said.

"That's my hard drive you were checking out, not my browser," Faith said.

"I've just ended the browsing bit," Luke said.

"You were snooping around as if you'd find something on me, weren't you?" she asked. "How dare you."

"It's not what it looks like," Luke said, trying to claw back some trust. But he knew he was grasping at straws.

Faith glared at him. "You come here pretending to be helping me, but this was your end game, wasn't it? I wouldn't be surprised if that so-called intruder is an actor you paid off to get in here, right?"

"That wasn't an act. He was breaking in…" Luke began.

"I don't give a damn. Get out of my house. Now!" Faith said.

"Don't do this," Luke said.

"It's already done. Get out or I'll call the cops," she warned.

Her fiery eyes made him see an edgy side to her he'd never experienced before. The rage in them was palpable, and its intensity concerned him.

Without another word, he walked out. The door slammed behind him, and he could hear all the safety latches applied with anger.

As he walked to his car, he wasn't sure if he'd blown it. If she was innocent, then she was now exposed to the thugs. If she'd killed Mark, then she'd probably send the thugs after him.

He needed to keep an eye over his shoulder.

20

————————

LUKE GOT into his car and, instead of leaving, he watched the house again, as if he expected another stranger to arrive and cause a disturbance. His wrists were starting to hurt again, and he knew it was from lack of sleep. However, an hour later, his eyelids became heavy, and he promptly slept.

The warm rays of the sun woke him up in the morning. Startled, he wiped his eyes and looked around him. The street was still inactive except for two people who were out jogging. He massaged his wrists, which were not as sore as he expected they would be.

Luke turned on his engine and pulled out of the car park. He drove along the highway, heading towards his motel. He craved a shower and fresh clothes, and thereafter a substantial breakfast to kick off the day.

He'd just got off the highway when he noticed an SUV that had been behind him for several kilometres. The road ahead was still pretty clear, and he knew it was a more powerful car.

When he slowed down considerably, instead of passing

him, it slowed down too. There was no denying it - he was being trailed.

By who? Had Faith already sounded the alarm, and now the thugs were onto her? Were they the police?

The reason he couldn't tell was because the car's windows were heavily tinted. The best he could do was see the driver's knuckles on the steering wheel.

Luke sped up hard, trying to eek out every bit of horse-power in his car. The SUV didn't let him pull away too far. In fact, it always easily caught up.

Suddenly, the SUV accelerated. Luke slowed down, expecting it to drive past. Instead of passing him, the SUV stayed alongside him. All side windows were also heavily tinted, so all he could see was the reflection of the clear sky. Luke wondered if it was a bunch of rich kids messing around with their parents' expensive car.

His questions were answered with a jolt as the SUV suddenly swerved to the left, striking his car on the right side. Luke grabbed the steering wheel with both hands to keep the car on the road.

But the SUV didn't want him to stay on the road, and hit him again. This time, Luke over-corrected his steering, and he was suddenly swerving left and right as the wheels squealed underneath him. He lost control and watched the car take a hard left, which took him off the tarmac.

Luke's car bounced over the uneven ground as it hurtled towards a clump of trees. Luke braked slowly, aware that a hard stop at high speed would cause him to roll.

"Come on, girl," he muttered under his breath.

He was carrying too much momentum to stop in time, and he braced himself. He angled his car towards one of the shorter trees with a thinner trunk and braced himself for impact.

The car slammed into the trunk, and he saw the whole dashboard move back towards him. The airbag came on instantly and he was engulfed in a white blur. His ears stung with a high-pitched sound.

The car had stopped.

Luke coughed and strained his neck to look around him. He reached for the door. It was jammed. Two shoves made it came loose. He threw himself to the ground and coughed some more. He started getting to his feet. From the corner of his eye, he could see men clad in black running towards him.

He egged himself on, rushing towards the trees. His left leg hurt just above the knee, and his chest had a growing soreness. He'd deal with that later. The priority was to get away.

But he wasn't moving fast enough. Even as he ran through trees and brushes, he could hear the footfalls behind him get closer.

Suddenly, the ground beneath him disappeared, and he was floating for a few seconds before he realised where he was as he landed hard at the bottom of an old hunter's pit. It was filled with earth and dead branches, so it wasn't as deep as it used to be. But he felt the impact smashing into the debris face first. His chest throbbed. He wiped off dead leaves and twigs from his face. As he turned to look up at the entrance, he heard voices approach.

He tried using a dead tree trunk to get himself out. As soon as his head was back on level ground, he saw two men running towards him. He would've ducked, but they had already spotted him.

"There he is," a bald man said. They got to him at the same time and pulled him out of the hole.

"What do you think you're doing? Do you know who you're running away from?" the other man asked.

"I've not done anything. Please, we can talk about this," Luke said.

"Talk about what?" the bald man retorted as he slapped Luke's left cheek. The energy made Luke's head cock sideways, and he lost his balance. The other man punched him in the gut. Luke fell to his knees as he absorbed the impact.

Kicks struck his sides as the men attacked him.

"Stop it guys!" a fresh voice shouted amidst the chaos.

"We need to teach him a lesson," the bald man replied.

"Stop, I know this man."

The blows stopped, and Luke opened one eye. He recognised Kabelo's cousin, Ndlovu.

"You know him from where?" the bald man asked.

"He's my uncle's friend," Ndlovu replied.

"Then why was he messing with Andile? He tried to rough him up at night," the bald man replied.

Ndlovu turned to Luke. "Why did you touch him?"

"You mean the guy who was trying to attack Faith? I just wanted to protect her. I didn't know why he was visiting her in the dead of the night," Luke said.

"He was there for a mission that was none of your business," the bald man said. "Unless you're trying to protect Mark. Were you in cahoots with him?"

"Cahoots about what?" Luke asked.

"Guys, let's take him to the boss. Do nothing crazy to him here," Ndlovu said.

The three men exchanged knowing glances.

"Good idea," the bald man said, lifting Luke to his feet. "You're coming with us."

"To where?" Luke asked.

"You're going to see the General. You and Mark owe him something that he wants returned," the bald man replied with a sly grin.

21

THEY DROVE Luke with his head held flat to the floor of the car. Along his right side, he could feel the weight of the feet of the three men who sat above him. This was the option they chose instead of using a blindfold, possibly to teach him a lesson for trying to escape. It was a smooth ride on the highways, so it was a mild consolation that he wasn't being taken deep into a forest.

He also silently hoped that, whoever the General was, he wouldn't overrule Ndlovu's intention to save his life. They soon stopped at a gate. Luke heard its metal hinges squeal as it opened and they drove in and the car finally came to a stop. The doors flew open. He reckoned the ride took close to forty minutes.

"Get out," one man ordered, and Luke lifted himself from the floor of the backseat. He gingerly got out of the car, feeling the soreness on every part of his frame.

Outside, he stepped on brown earth. Around him was open, scorched land. In the distance, he could see large mounds of earth next to deep, excavated holes. This was an abandoned quarry, Luke concluded.

Closer to him, he saw a structure built out of iron sheet and timber. It was fairly new, akin to a site office at a construction site. Its singular door and two windows were open. The door had two men seated on either side of it. Although they didn't show it, he knew they were armed.

"Let's go," one of the bald men said, nudging him forward.

Ndlovu hurried to Luke's side to make sure someone did not further harass him as they approached the structure. The two men at the door got to their feet as they closed in.

They entered the structure, and the darker interior made Luke's eyes take a few seconds to adjust to the light change.

It was a single room office, with a wooden desk and a tall chair like that of a traditional chief propped up against the wall. A bench was placed on the opposite side of the table.

A tall, sinewy man in a green beret, a makeshift military uniform and sunglasses occupied the traditional seat. He had a short green stick dangling from the corner of his mouth.

"He's here, General," the bald man said.

The General stood up and smiled. His towering figure almost hit the roof rafters.

"Welcome to our little office, Luke," the General said, pointing at the bench. "You can have a seat after such a long drive to visit me."

Luke hobbled to the bench and sat down. The General propped himself on the front of the table and studied Luke's frame until he started fidgeting.

"What are you doing here?" the General asked.

"I'm wondering the same thing," Luke replied.

"Let me rephrase. Why did you attack one of my men?" the General said.

"I didn't know he was one of your men. I just saw him outside the house of a friend and I defended her," Luke replied.

"Do you normally watch your friend's homes around midnight?" he asked.

"It had been a late visit," Luke replied.

"Don't lie. She's not really a friend, is she?" the General asked.

Luke gave him nothing. The General walked to one window. He chewed on his stick, bit off a piece, and spat it out.

"You lost your business recently and you've opened this makeshift outfit you call a private investigator agency. You're still learning your way around the streets, but somehow you've solved a few cases. However, you came very close to death the night you attacked one of my men and you hardly realise that," the General said. "Yes, I know a few things about you. But my key question today is this: Do you believe life is a rehearsal, Luke?"

The General walked back to the table.

"Look at me when I speak to you," the General hissed.

Luke lifted his head until they locked eyes.

"Do you, Luke Mbeki, believe life is a rehearsal?"

"No, I don't," Luke replied.

"Neither do I. Everything I do is intentional. Every seed I plant has to bear fruit. Mark has something that belongs to me, and people like you think they can stop me from taking it back," the General said as he moved closer to Luke. "You'd better give me a good reason why I shouldn't tell one of my men to end your life."

"He didn't know what he was doing, boss," Ndlovu interjected. "He's just trying to solve Mark's murder."

"Why do you want to stand up for him?" the General asked.

"Because Kabelo works for him. You know my uncle, right?" Ndlovu said.

The General mulled over this new piece of information.

"Kabs is part of his crew? Then he should be more street smart than he is now," the General said, backing away.

"I'm trying my best," Luke said. "And I'm sorry for the misunderstanding. If you share with me what arrangements you had with Mark, it will help me catch his killer."

"I also want to know who killed him because I've lost a lot of money. No one knows where he buried my stash," the General said.

"What stash are we talking about?" Luke asked.

The General stared at Ndlovu. "Like I said, he needs your uncle to teach him to be street smart."

"I think being street smart involves building trust. This is me keeping it real," Luke said.

The General stared at Luke for a moment before nodding. "Fair enough. Mark would make private deliveries for me. Things that are high-value goods in the black market. We've done this for years."

"Do you know anyone in the business who would want him dead?" Luke asked.

"We kept our communications discreet to avoid that. I have enemies, but I don't think they'd come for him instead of me or my men. We have some level of respect in this business," the General replied.

"I understand that. The reason I was there last night is part of my investigation. So, in case you have something about Mark that could help, I'd appreciate it," Luke said.

"I always suspected he'd use one of his women to hide some of these things. Safe houses, they're called. But now that I think about it, I've lost more by the simple fact Mark is dead. Who's gonna do our runs now?" the General mused.

No one responded.

"That silence is the sound of loss," the General said. "We've lost a gem in Mark. Find whoever did this, and I'll forgive his debt."

Luke turned to him. "Can I hold you to your word?"

"Yes, you can."

Luke nodded. "Does that mean I can leave now?"

The General bit another piece off his stick, walked to a window and spat it out.

"You can leave. I hear your car is a little damaged. Don't go looking for it. Give it two weeks, and it will be back in your hands. Okay?" the General said.

Luke scratched the back of his head. "Okay. Thank you. Can I get a ride?"

"Ndlovu will get you sorted. Just remember to find this person," the General said.

"I will, sir," Luke replied.

Ndlovu drove Luke in one of the tinted SUVs. They reached the edge of the city centre and he was dropped off.

"Stay safe. I'll be in touch about the car," Ndlovu said.

"Thanks for helping today. I owe you one," Luke replied as he got out.

Once on the sidewalk, Luke looked around. It was nearing rush hour in the evening, and people were filling the bus stops as they prepared to head home.

Home was the last thing on Luke's mind. He needed to think things through after the whirlwind of experiences he'd had in the last 24 hours. He took a taxi minibus to the office. When he got there, he found Cindi still working on her computer.

"I was wondering where you were," Cindi said as she watched him walk in.

"Long story. Plus, my phone has been off for a few hours," Luke said as he switched on his mobile phone. He noted the battery was low. "Anything new while I was away?"

"Well, I thought of tracking how Mark booked his plane ticket. It turns out he didn't do it himself, but an employee of his did. His name is Herman. He works as one of the couriers," Cindi replied.

"That's good. When do we talk to him?" Luke said.

"I already did. He says Mark told him to make the booking because he was running late to deliver a package to a VIP client called Miss Doe," Cindi replied.

"Miss Doe? As in Jane Doe?" Luke asked.

"I wondered the same thing. But the record simply says Miss Doe. But a good guess is her first name is Jane," Cindi said.

"And we both know that's not her real name," he said. "But we can now say for sure it's a woman who sent him on this fatal treasure hunt."

"Fatal treasure hunt," Cindi said, staring at the ceiling. "Sounds like a novel title. But yes, it's definitely a woman. Or a man who wants to confuse the investigators. You never know."

"True, but whoever did it knew him well, considering they bought him a gun that he'd always craved to have in his collection," Luke said.

"The bait was well-thought out," Cindi said.

"The more I think about it, the more I feel it's a pro who did this killing," Luke said, stroking his chin.

His phone rang. It was his mother.

"Ma, is everything okay?" Luke asked.

"I've been looking for you all day. How are you, son?" Mable asked.

"I'm fine, Ma. Talk to me," Luke said.

"I wanted you to visit me today," Mable replied.

"Is it urgent?" Luke asked.

"You don't want to see your mother now when she calls you? I remember when you were younger, and I'd call you from the next room you'd always come running. Now that you're big, I don't matter anymore?" Mable said.

Luke rubbed his temple. "You matter, Ma. You always have and always will. If it's not that urgent, can we do tomorrow? At least I can create more time to spend with you instead of rushing there today."

Mable sighed. "Okay, but make sure you come tomorrow. It's important."

"I will, Ma. Trust me," Luke said.

He hung up and looked up at Cindi. "We need to follow up this Miss Doe thing."

"How do we do that?" Cindi asked.

"We lay bait. I have a hunch this might be Faith's doing. She's smart, had a bone to pick with Mark and his wife, and she had the means to pay someone to do it for her. She might have been misdirecting on purpose to remove all traces connecting it back to her," Luke said.

Cindi leaned forward with a puzzled expression. "How do you plan to do this?"

"Using her nemesis Lynda as bait," Luke replied with a smile.

22

LUKE SAT at his desk and called Lynda.

"You've got an update for me?" Lynda asked. "It's been a while since I got one of those."

"Sorry for the silence. It's been busy the last few days. But we've made some headway," Luke said.

"That sounds good. Tell me more," she replied.

"I want to do that, but I think I should brief you in person," he said.

"This sounds interesting."

"It is. I'll give you all the details when we meet," Luke said. "When are you available?"

Lynda went silent for a few seconds. Luke could hear the flipping of pages in the background. Cindi, seated across from him, waited with bated breath as she sipped a mug of hot chocolate.

"The coming days are pretty full at the moment. How about we do dinner tonight?" Lynda asked.

"Dinner sounds fine. I could take you out to a restaurant I like," Luke said.

"I was thinking you could come over to my place. I'll make you dinner," Lynda replied.

Luke nodded and gave Cindi the thumbs up. "Alright, that can work. I'll be there around seven?"

"Seven works for me. See you then," Lynda said.

"See you." Luke hung up and leaned back in his chair with a smug look. "The plan is on."

"Nice. What's your plan for nailing Faith, though? And how will you convince Lynda to play along?" Cindi asked.

"It's still quite rough in my mind, but I was thinking of setting up a meeting between the two of them. I'll feed Lynda with the questions I'd like her to ask Faith. Each question will push the edge closer to accusing Faith. We both know how she has a short fuse," Luke said.

"And Lynda rattles her," Cindi added.

"Exactly. If she loses her mind, she will spill out information she didn't want to be known. Then I'll take it from there," Luke said.

"So Lynda's going to wear a wire?" Cindi asked.

"Something like that," Luke said.

"Come on, Luke..." Cindi began before Luke's ringing phone cut her off.

"Hello, Ma. Remembered something?" Luke said.

"Hello, son. I still want you to visit me, but it can't wait till tomorrow," Mable said.

Luke was now suspicious. This was unlike her.

"Ma, what's going on with you?" Luke asked. "My schedule today is a little crazy."

"Son, if I was unwell, would it be a matter of fitting me into your schedule?" Mable asked.

"I'm sorry, Ma. I didn't mean it that way," Luke said. He glanced at his wristwatch. "I'll pass by in half an hour."

"Thank you. I look forward to seeing you," Mable replied.

Luke let out a sigh as he got up. "I wanted to charge this phone, but I'll have to do it on the go."

"Is everything okay?" Cindi asked.

"I hope so. My mother wants to see me urgently, and I've been a bit too casual about it. Anyway, I'll let you know how it goes with Lynda," Luke said as he made for the door.

He was grateful when he dodged all the evening traffic and arrived at his mother's house in less than half an hour. She met him at the door with a beaming smile.

"You've become very hard to find," Mable said.

"It's not like that, Ma. You know I'm only a phone call away," Luke replied. He hugged her.

"That was more than one phone call that finally got you here," she said as she ushered him in.

Inside, the house was as he always remembered it: neat, warm and with the aroma of her cooking wafting through every room in the house. There was always something in the kitchen. However, there was one new thing that he'd never seen before. It was in the form of a woman in her thirties seated on the couch. She wore a long, colourful dress which bore hints of Xhosa traditional patterns on the hem. On her head was a headscarf that masked her lush afro hair. She had a pleasant smile and wide, curious eyes.

"Rose, this is my son, Luke. Luke, this is my friend, Rose," Mable said.

Rose stood up and shook Luke's hand. Her hand was tender to the touch.

"Nice to meet you, Luke. Your mother has told me a lot about you," Rose said in a silky, yet confident manner.

"Has she now? I hope it's all been good?" Luke said.

"Mostly good," Rose replied.

"Have a seat, no point in talking like pedestrians on the street," Mable said.

Rose went back to the couch, while Luke sat on the single-seater across from her. Mable sat on the couch's arm.

"Are you okay, Ma?" Luke asked.

"I'm well. We thank the Lord. He always keeps me young and energetic," Mable replied.

"I'm glad to hear that. You had me worried," Luke said as he checked his phone. It was about to go off. He took out the charger in his pocket.

"You want to charge that?" Mable asked. "You know where the socket is. Let me finish making the tea."

Mable rose. As she walked to the kitchen, she stopped by the wall unit and turned on the radio. The sounds of Ladysmith Black Mambazo's 'Shosholoza' filtered through the room. She disappeared into the kitchen, doing a light jig as she sang along.

Luke stood and walked to the wall unit. Next to the radio was an extension cord. He switched off his phone, connected the charger, and plugged it into the extension.

He hoped he'd at least get twenty minutes' worth of charge before he left for Lynda's place. He needed to stay in touch with Cindi.

Luke walked back to the chair and sat down. He kept fidgeting, checking the wall clock, and adjusting the seat cover as he waited. His mind wandered to the case. He played out the diner with Lynda in his mind and rehearsed the words he'd use to convince her to plot a ruse to trap Faith.

"Would you like the music a little louder?" Rose asked.

"What?" Luke replied, startled out of his train of thoughts.

"The music. Would you like it louder?" Rose repeated.

"Er, no. Ladysmith have voices that carry well across the space," Luke said.

"Well, it doesn't sound like you're enjoying the music," Rose said.

Luke smiled. "I'm listening to it. Grew up with it so it's been part of the family. I'm comfortable with it."

"You look lost in another world," Rose said.

"I've got a few things on my mind," he replied.

"Sounds like a man with many distractions," Rose said.

"Distractions?" he asked.

"Yes, things that make you take detours you wouldn't normally take," Rose said.

Luke was impressed by how intuitive she was.

"Something like that. But isn't that the journey of life? Sometimes you've got to adjust to new realities," Luke said.

He checked his wristwatch, wondering why his mother's tea was taking so long. She'd been gone for nearly half an hour. It was inching towards half-past six, and soon it would be dark outside.

"Give me a moment," Luke said as he rose and walked to the kitchen. There, he found his mother slowly stirring a pot of milk tea. He checked the heat, and it was set to medium.

"Ma, why is the heat set to medium yet you know I'm leaving soon?" Luke asked.

She smiled as she turned to him. "You've always been impatient. Do you want freshly made tea or burnt tea?"

"We've made tea on that cooker for over ten years at high heat and it's never been burnt," Luke said.

"But it's older now, and can't handle those high pressures you're so used to," Mable replied.

Luke shook his head. He lowered his voice. "You're doing

this intentionally, aren't you? You left us alone to talk for all that time."

"At least you're not as blind as I thought you were," she said.

Luke sighed. He feigned a smile and shook his head. "I'm sorry, Ma."

Mable raised a brow. "What for?"

"I've got to go. I'll have to come back for the tea later," Luke said as he turned away.

"What do you mean later?" Mable said, her voice trailing off behind him.

Luke went straight to where he was charging his phone and unplugged it. He hoped the charge would last him at least two hours.

"You're leaving?" Rose asked.

"Unfortunately," Luke replied.

"I was just getting to know you," Rose said.

He turned to her, and they locked eyes. "You knew what she was up to, didn't you?"

Rose nodded. "I've never done this before either, if that helps."

Luke nodded. "Oddly, it does. This was interesting."

"Maybe we'll meet again under different circumstances," Rose said.

"Maybe," Luke said. In the back of his mind, he thought of asking for her number, but that he was doing it in his mother's house felt strange to him. So he chose not to.

As he rushed to the door, Mable appeared in front of him, holding a tumbler flask and a jar of *biltong*. She handed them to him.

"You can't leave your mother's house without tasting her cooking. I want you to stay in my blessing, my son," Mable said.

Luke smiled, took the package, and kissed her on the cheek. "Thank you, Ma. We'll talk soon."

"The one you need to talk to right now is still in the living room," Mable said.

"Not now, Ma," Luke said.

He left the house, his mind quickly calculating how much traffic he needed to dodge to get to Lynda's house.

This plan needed to work, and nothing was going to hold him back.

23

———

Luke jumped into his car and drove off fast towards Lynda's house. The only detour he made was to stop over at a service station to buy a bottle of wine. They had little variety, so he hoped the gesture would mask the cheap wine he'd bought.

He arrived fifteen minutes late. When she opened the door, she smiled at him in quiet amusement.

"I'm sorry for my lateness. I had to pass by my Mom's place," Luke said.

"That's fine. Come on in. I was just getting ready to serve," she replied as she walked away.

He followed her, the pleasant scent of spicy food wafting to his nostrils. The house was warm, so he took off his coat.

"Down this way," Lynda said. They went down a corridor lined with potted plants. On the walls were various items from traditional Zulu history—shields, spears and swords.

"Someone loves Zulu tradition," Luke remarked.

Lynda chuckled. "That's Mark's thing. He's really into Zulu history and their warring prowess."

Belatedly, Luke remembered to switch on his phone. It soon started vibrating with incoming messages.

They entered the dining room. It was oval-shaped and had five seats around the dining table.

"Please settle in and get comfortable. I'll be right back," Lynda said.

"Thanks," Luke said.

He looked around the room. There were windows on every side except two: the one that led to the kitchen, and the other wall that had a wine cabinet. For a fleeting moment, he was tempted to check if the bottle in his hand measured up to those in the cabinet. He set the bottle atop the dining table and sat down.

As he relaxed, he could hear the soft sound of jazz music filtering from the kitchen.

Lynda emerged with two steaming bowls. As she set them down, Luke saw their contents and his stomach grumbled in expectation: grilled chicken and glazed potatoes.

"Just a moment as I get the salad," Lynda said.

Luke took out his phone and started checking his messages. One was from Cindi.

About Lynda and the pottery class. She...

"Sorry to keep you waiting," Lynda said as she returned after a few seconds with a third bowl full of fresh salad.

Luke looked up and smiled. "You're hardly breaking a sweat. Sometimes the wait is worth it."

"*Jabulela ukudla kwakho,*" Lynda said. "Enjoy your meal."

"You speak Zulu although you're Xhosa," Luke said.

"Like I said, Mark is a fan, and I just went with the flow," Lynda said.

They both served the meal and Luke was so famished he wasted no time digging in. The flavours in his mouth were heavenly.

"You prepared a feast for the gods," Luke said with a smile.

"Are you trying to flatter me?" Lynda asked.

"I'm not trying. This is blatant flattery without apology. This is fantastic," Luke replied.

Lynda blushed. "Thank you. I'm glad you like it."

Luke's phone vibrated again. It was Cindi.

Please read my last text and let me know if you understand asap.

"You're still working even now?" Lynda asked.

Luke smiled. "I'm always on the clock. Especially when having dinner with my client."

He found Cindi's last text.

About Lynda and the pottery class. She was an hour late to the class. Her shoes had some red mud, similar to that from the shooting range.

Luke felt his throat dry. He grabbed a glass of water and drank it all.

"How are the potatoes?" Lynda asked. "It's my first harvest from my little garden in the back."

Luke nodded and smiled. "They are delicious. I'm not sure if it's just the harvest or the way you roasted them, but these are some of the best I've had in a long time."

Even as he said this, only one thought was going through his mind: the killer needed less than an hour at the shooting range.

Lynda blushed. "Maybe it's a combination of both?"

"Oh, the full package? Then it's a perfect ten in my book."

They both laughed.

Luke was surprised by his composure, but he was getting better at buying time. His mind was racing, trying to figure out how to manoeuvre the conversation. If his hunches were right, then he was having dinner with Mark's killer, not the bait. He hadn't prepared for this.

"Something interesting came up with the case the other day. We found out that one of Mark's employees booked the air ticket," Luke said.

Lynda frowned. "Really? Why? He was always keen on that to make sure he got a window seat."

"Apparently, he was delivering a VIP package to a lady calling herself Miss Doe. Does she sound familiar?" Luke asked, studying her reaction.

Lynda shook her head, avoiding eye contact. "I have no idea."

"Yeah, it was a clever choice of names. But it got me thinking that maybe it's someone whose background was in the medical field or the disciplined forces, that kind of thing."

Lynda shrugged. "That's an interesting idea. Did you make any headway with it?"

"Not really. It's still a very broad assumption," Luke replied. "But I found something else when I went to the pottery class."

Lynda's hand froze with a fork in mid-air, with a piece of roasted potato dripping with gravy.

"Why did you go there?" she asked.

"You had said that you used to go there with Mark, and I wanted to find out if he enjoyed the sessions or not," Luke said.

"And what did you find out?"

"He struggled a lot more than I did when I was there," Luke said with a smile.

Lynda feigned a smile and wiped her mouth with a table napkin.

"Would you like some wine?" she asked.

"I bought you a bottle," Luke said, pointing at the one he'd arrived with.

"Thanks. There's one I'd wanted you to try out, though," Lynda said.

Before he could respond, she'd already got up and walked to him. She took his glass and walked to the wine cabinet behind him. He heard her pop open the bottle.

"They also told me that although you attended the class that day, you also arrived an hour late. Something that had never happened before. Did you have car trouble?" Luke asked.

He heard the wine pour into his glass as she spoke.

"It was a mix of traffic and a late departure. I ran late. I even called to let them know. They told you that, right?" Lynda said.

"Yeah, they did," Luke said.

He heard her walking towards him and turned to his right, just in time to see the shadow on the floor of a wine bottle speeding towards his head. He ducked, lying flat on the table, and heard the whoosh of the bottle over his ear.

He pushed back his chair, slamming into her and causing Lynda to retreat. But it was a temporary reprieve as she came after him again with the bottle. This time, he lifted the dinner chair and watched the bottle smash into a million pieces as it impacted the chair's legs.

She grabbed the chair from him with surprising strength, tossing it to the side.

"Lynda, what's going on?" Luke asked.

"I should ask you the same question," Lynda said as she moved in.

She swung a right hook and then a left in quick succession. He ducked the first, but the left hook landed square on his temple. The blow sent him hurtling towards the dinner table, knocking over some more dinner chairs along the way. He shook his head and kept himself upright. He back tracked as he watched her approach, guiding himself towards the corridor that led to the living room.

"Where did you learn to do that?" Luke asked.

"I had a military grandfather. Then I got married to a man who loves guns. You thought I wouldn't know how to defend myself?" Lynda said as she walked towards him.

Luke kept backtracking down the corridor, occasionally looking behind him to avoid the flower vases that lined up along the walls.

"Defend yourself against what? What's this about?" Luke asked.

"This life isn't a game, Luke. Everyone has an agenda. Anyone is out to get you. I thought you were in my corner in this case," Lynda said.

"I am. You're my client," Luke said.

"Who are you working for? Because the questions you're asking me are those an enemy would ask, not a friend," Lynda said.

As she passed a wall installation of ancient Zulu weapons, she paused and reached for one. She held an *assegai* by the shaft, a short stabbing spear. Its long blade reflected the overhead corridor light as she swung it through the air in short bursts, as if mimicking Shaka Zulu's prowess. This sent a chill down Luke's spine.

He turned to glance behind him in panic, but he was a moment too late. His foot struck a vase, sending him toppling to the floor. He tried getting up but his knees felt like jelly, and slipped. He pushed himself backwards, but she was closing in.

"You should've just followed the leads with Faith and George. We wouldn't be here tonight," Lynda said as she raised the *assegai* up in the air, her eyes glinting with the colour of death.

24

Luke kept moving back, but Lynda's shadow was already towering over him. He watched her raise the weapon and his flight instinct switched to fight.

He glanced at the floor and saw the rug Lynda stood on. With all he had left, he gave it a hard yank, hoping it wasn't taped to the floor. He was in luck.

The rug responded to his pull, coming off the floor. He kept pulling with all his might. He saw the surprise on Lynda's face as the ground beneath her moved, and her hands flailed in the air. The next thing he heard was Lynda's body thud onto the wooden floor. The clank of the *assegai* followed as it flew from her hands, skidding across the corridor.

Luke didn't have a moment to waste. He sprung towards her stricken form and before she could reach for the *assegai*, he was atop her, her arms in his vice-like grip.

"Stop it, it's over," he said to her as she struggled to release herself.

"Let go of me," she said as she fought back.

This struggle for control went on for a few more minutes until she got tired.

"Let me go and we can talk," Lynda said.

"The only thing I want you to tell me is why you did it," Luke replied.

Lynda laughed. "You wouldn't understand the truth, even if it stood in front of you."

"Try me," he said.

"I didn't do it," Lynda said. "We're all part of a grand scheme."

"What grand scheme?" Luke asked.

"You'll have to let me go to hear it," Lynda replied.

Luke shook his head. "Did you hear me when I told you it's over? Can you hear that?"

He tilted his head. In the distance, the approaching sounds of wailing sirens could be heard.

"That's not an ambulance. They're coming here for you," Luke said. "The sooner you can get me on your side, the better. Right now, you're doing it wrong."

"Like I told you. I didn't do it. The General did," Lynda said, her eyes filled with desperation.

"I'm not listening to any of this. You had your chance," Luke said.

Ten minutes later, Lynda's house was surrounded, with blue and red flashes splashing onto the interior walls.

The police came in and arrested Lynda. As they did this, they also took Luke outside as they investigated the scene. An officer asked him what happened, and he explained to him the evening's events, including Lynda's surprise attack.

Once done, the officer went and briefed Detective Tony, who had been overseeing the collection of evidence. His partner Detective Shozi was present, but all she did was give Luke a distant look of disdain.

Detective Tony tapped the officer's shoulder in mild approval and approached Luke.

"You're making this a habit, aren't you?" Detective Tony asked, smiling. He sat next to Luke.

"I don't know what to say. I keep finding myself in these situations," Luke replied.

"Or they keep finding you. You're riding your luck, you know," the detective said.

"To be honest, this time you're right. She could've ended me in there. She kept leading me on until the very last moment," Luke said.

"From what you told my officer, she can use that assegai well," Detective Tony said. "You're lucky to be here."

"Trust me, I know that," Luke said. "I'm no macho man."

"So she was Miss Doe, the lady who set up the treasure hunt for her husband to follow? Through another lens, one could call that romantic," Detective Tony said.

"She did. Lynda had plotted things to mesh together, including the murder and her alibi. She knew she'd be attending the pottery class. Her mistake was running very late to the class, an unusual occurrence. Otherwise, her alibi was strong enough," Luke said. "In a strange way, Mark did us that favour. He left the hotel late, which made him arrive at the shooting range later than she'd have wanted."

"Then she killed him with his own gift," Detective Tony said.

"Unfortunately so," Luke replied.

Just then, Lynda was led outside to a waiting police car. Behind her, two detectives carried evidence bags with pieces of the broken wine bottle and the *assegai*. Luke and the detective watched as Lynda struggled with the two officers that were leading her.

"You're making a mistake!" Lynda kept saying even as they forced her into the backseat of the police car.

"That's a woman who's lost all sense of reality," Detective Tony muttered.

"I think she plotted this for months," Luke said. "She studied his patterns and routine. Being his wife, she, of course, knew of his love for guns, and his shooting range routine. I think it's even possible Mark knew it was her who was leading him on with the treasure hunt. We'll never know."

"I've always wondered why he'd deliver to an abandoned shooting range," Detective Tony said. "I think he's done these shady location drop offs before."

Luke nodded. "I think you're right. He's received strange customer requests, and unusual drop off locations were the norm. So long as there was money to be made."

"So the gun was a gift, something he craved. Why the symbolism?" the detective asked.

"It was one of those collectible pieces that Mark had always wanted. I think now that she was angry with him for something. Maybe she found out that he was cheating. Killing him with his gift was the ultimate revenge. She then went to the pottery class as if nothing happened," Luke said. "She hoped to use George and Faith as her fall guys."

"She was feeding you clues?" Detective Tony asked.

"Yeah. She was my client, and I didn't think that she'd be manipulating me. She was just a grieving wife in need of justice," Luke said.

"Did she tell you why she did it?" the detective asked.

Luke shook his head. "She kept saying she didn't do it."

Detective Tony sighed. "I'll have to talk to her downtown."

"Will you let me know how it goes?" Luke asked.

Detective Tony gave him a sideways look. "We'll see. I still have to get physical evidence it was her, along with a confession. At the moment, all we have is that she attacked you tonight. That can keep her in custody for a few days. So if there's anything else connecting her to the murder that you have, you'd better share it with me."

"I will. Thanks for the help today," Luke said.

"Thank those two, not me," the detective said as he pointed at Cindi and Kabelo, who stood watching from a distance.

The detective rose to leave. "Stay away from people who want you dead. Human nature isn't always forgiving."

Detective Tony walked off, giving room for Cindi and Kabelo to walk up to Luke. They embraced.

"Thanks guys. You've got no idea how close that was," Luke said.

"It's over now?" Cindi asked.

"No, it's not. If Lynda doesn't confess, we have a problem on our hands," Luke said.

25

———————

FOR THE MANY months he'd been living in a motel, Luke had fantasied about living in a house with a balcony. The urge for freedom became too strong, and although his finances were yet to improve, he'd already moved out.

His new home was a nice two-bedroomed apartment off the Highway 8. The Walrus Apartments compound had more concrete than trees, but he needed an escape and this was it. He'd convinced Cindi and used some office cash to get basic furniture. Kabelo had insisted they needed to do a housewarming, which is why, on this Saturday afternoon in a half-empty house, Luke was hosting Cindi, Kabelo and a few other friends.

Amapiano music was blaring from Kabelo's portable music system.

Luke, decked in a Hawaiian shirt and khaki shorts, was grilling burger patties and chicken breasts on the balcony as he heard the lively conversation going on inside.

"*Brah,* do you want a drink?" Kabelo kept asking every few minutes. He performed a little jig as he did this, although Luke knew this was a ploy to see what meat was done.

"Drinks and the fire don't work well together, Kabs. Help me put these burgers together," Luke instructed.

"My pleasure," Kabelo said as he rolled up his sleeves and positioned himself at an adjacent serving table.

"Kabs, that's not how you do burgers!" Cindi protested as she emerged from behind the living room curtain.

"What do you mean? It's meat, bun, meat, bun? It's not complicated," Kabelo said.

"Where are the greens?" Cindi asked.

"Ask the host," Kabelo said.

"I didn't get any," Luke replied.

Cindi shook her head. "I told you to get a girlfriend."

"*Eish,* be easy. I've been trying to stay live," Luke replied. "You can go to the grocery lady downstairs. She's got a few, I'm sure."

"Kabs, you do that run. I'll take over here," Cindi said as she pushed him out of his station.

"Luke, you see what's happening?" Kabelo said.

"Just do it, Kabs. By the time you get back, you'll have plenty of food to eat," Luke said.

Kabelo left, muttering under his breath. Luke and Cindi laughed.

"The other food is almost ready. The rice, meat stew, lamb, chicken curry, the works. But he seems to want the burgers more," Cindi said.

"He loves a good *braai,* so I can't blame him," Luke said. "Thanks for helping set this up. I needed it after the week we've had."

"You're welcome. Any word from the cops?" Cindi asked.

"Yeah. Detective Tony called this morning with some good

news," Luke said. "Lynda's case is a done deal, although she refused to confess or show remorse. A street CCTV camera caught her meeting the courier who delivered the package to the hotel. But what really nailed her was the fact the couple who run the pawn shop pointed her out in an identification parade. The police could finally link her with the gun. The court hearing starts in two weeks, so I'll be taking the stand. She's going away for life at the bare minimum."

"That's great. I was worried that despite her blunders she was going to get away with it," Cindi said.

"She sure put up a fight. Did you look into her background a little more?" Luke asked.

"Yeah. It's true that she spent a lot of time with her ex-military grandfather when she was younger, and I suspect he taught how to defend herself," Cindi said.

"You know what?" Luke said. "You were right about her."

"I was right?"

"You warned me she was distracting me. My blind spot almost got me killed," Luke said.

"Glad that you realised eventually," Cindi said with a wink. "What happens to Mark's company now?"

"They'll shut down. Mark was the glue, and the discreet services were all about trust. There's no one to do it anymore. Maybe it's a good thing, because I think it was only a matter of time before one of those secret packages got them on the wrong side of the law," Luke said.

"Are the gang still going after Mark's relatives? You know it might affect Faith," Cindi asked.

"No, we got that sorted. Kabelo's cousin Ndlovu helped us get on the General's good side. He promised to waive Mark's debt if we caught the killer, and he'll honour his word. Faith is still angry that she was even a suspect. She wishes Mark had never married Lynda. Anyway, now she has nothing to worry about except raising her son," Luke said.

"How's he taking it?" Cindi asked.

"Not too well, but he'll get through it. It's the card that life has dealt. Faith just needs to be there for him," Luke said.

"Yeah. Is George getting some help?" Cindi said.

Luke shrugged as he turned over some patties. "Last time we spoke, he said he was still in therapy and had just got to the second round of an interview at a taxi company."

"At least he's trying to move on," Cindi said.

"Fingers crossed he pulls through," Luke said.

Cindi sighed. "So, we'll never know why she did this?"

Luke shook his head. "We might never know. I think she was tired of living with Mark. I think it was about his love for other women. The way she killed him was too personal. She wanted a clean slate on her own terms."

"Not being sure sounds a little bland for such an elaborate plan," Cindi said.

"Like Detective Tony said, she's created her own reality in her mind. Whatever was going on in that marriage, only she knows how important being free from Mark was. But she wanted it, and doesn't regret what she did," Luke said.

Just then, Kabelo returned with a bag full of fresh lettuce.

"Now it's time to feast," he said with a beaming smile.

The party went on till late that night, something that Luke hadn't done in years. The pile of dishes, plastic cups and empty bottles didn't matter that much. He felt loved.

The next day, with two bags filled with pots of leftover food, Luke drove to Queen's apartment. He'd told her he was on his way, so when he knocked, she didn't hesitate this time. Instead, she had a warm smile.

"What are those?" she asked, looking at the bags.

"I had a party yesterday and had too much food to eat. So I thought I'd share some of it with you," Luke said as he strode in.

He placed the bags on the floor and took out the pots.

"Now that you don't have any table, I guess we'll have the meal here?" he asked.

Queen, whose hands were covering her mouth in shock, raised a brow. "You want to eat now?"

"Yeah, let's have a bite. It extends the party, right?" Luke said.

Queen rushed to the kitchen and returned with two plates and some cutlery. Luke served the chicken curry, rice and a burger for both of them.

He smiled as he he watched her expression.

"It's been a while, huh?" he asked. She nodded.

They ate as Luke updated her on how things went with the case, giving only the key details she needed to know.

After they both got stuffed with all the tasty food, they sat sipping some juice.

"I don't know what to say," Queen said after a long silence.

"You don't have to say anything. It's life. You have nothing to worry about now. Just focus on pursuing your goals," Luke said. "As I said, if you need anything, I'm just a phone call away."

"Thanks. For everything," Queen said.

They kept talking for a while as Queen shared her plans and ambitions. Luke offered advice where he could, trying his best to build a new bond of friendship. He wanted her to make something of herself.

Later, as he walked down the dimly lit hallway of the

apartments on his way home, Luke felt content. He'd lifted someone's spirits, and it had returned his faith in humanity.

His phone rang as he got near to the flight of stairs. Glancing at the screen, it was a strange number. He hesitated, then took the call.

"Hello?" Luke said.

"Hello, Luke," a strange tenor voice said. "Long time no see. Are you ready to play some hide-and-seek one more time? This time, we can raise the stakes a little. Whoever loses the game also loses their life. How does that sound?"

The End

AFTERWORD

Thank you for reading Road to Disaster. I really hope you enjoyed reading it as much as I had writing it!

If you have a minute, please consider leaving a review on Amazon or the retailer where you got it.

Many thanks in advance for your support!

WESTBAY CITY MYSTERY SERIES
END OF THE ROAD

AVA ZUMA

ALSO BY AVA ZUMA

The Westbay City Mystery Series

End of the Road

Road to Disaster

Bump in the Road

Hit the Road

Road to Recovery

The Sunshine Cove Cozy Mystery Series

Makeup and Mayhem

Eyebrows and Evil Looks

Nails and Nightmare

Highlighters and Upheaval

Christmas Carols and Lipstick Perils

Foundation and Temptations